Tegan drove so fast going home she didn't have time to think about anything else except not getting a ticket. She knew a cop would have no idea what she had on under her shorts and tee shirt, but she didn't want to chance anyone finding out what a wanton woman she really was. When she got home, she found Rosa watching TV in the living room, and the kids all asleep upstairs. Since they frequently stayed over at each others' houses, this wasn't anything unusual. So she paid Rosa for the babysitting and sent her home, watching from her front porch until she saw Rosa enter her own front door.

She went upstairs to peek in on the kids and found the girls were indeed asleep, but the boys were still playing the computer games they loved. She told them to turn it off and get to sleep. They complained, but since both of them were yawning while they argued, she figured they'd turn in soon, and she left them to go fill her bathtub with water.

She was soaking in a bubble bath with a glass of wine in her hand and candles lit all around the room, when her cell phone rang. Since she was expecting the call; she had it on a chair next to the tub.

"Hello, Patti?"

"No, it's me," Alexander's low voice made her feel like her bones were melting. "Have dinner with me tomorrow night?"

"No! I can't get a sitter on such short notice!"

"The night after that?"

"*No!*"

"When?"

"Never! I told you, it's not going to happen again! Goodnight, Alex." She hung up the phone.

Alexander smiled at the phone in his hand. "Ah, but it *is* going to happen again. The only thing you can negotiate with me is where and when."

Wings ePress, Inc.

Edited by: Christie Kraemer
Copy Edited by: Jeanne Howard
Senior Editor: Lorraine Stephens
Managing Editor: Christie Kraemer
Executive Editor: Lorraine Stephens
Cover Artist: Richard Strooud

Wings ePress Books
http://www.wings-press.com

Copyright © 2009 by Fiona Gierzynski
ISBN 978-1-59705-641-0

Published In the United States Of America

April 2009

Wings ePress Inc.
403 Wallace Court
Richmond, KY 40475

NEVER TOO OLD FOR TH
GAME OF LOVE

Fiona McGier

A Wings ePress, Inc.

Encore L'AmourNovel

Dedication

To Carol, who suggested I write about someone "our" age.
And to Paul, my inspiration.

One

"He wants a *what* at the party?" Tegan yelped into the phone.

Patti laughed. "Yup, I figured that's how you'd react. Hey, you're not driving, are you?"

Tegan swerved to avoid the car that had just pulled in front of her, and swore under her breath at people who drive while talking on the phone and then use that as their excuse to *not* pay attention.

"Yeah, I'm driving, but I'm still paying attention, unlike that creep who just missed hitting me; and even though I've just heard the most unreasonable demand for a party that I can imagine! Where the hell does he expect us to be able to get a stripper from, and on such short notice?"

"I don't know, and I don't think he cares. He just called a few minutes ago, and as soon as I got off the phone with him, I called you. You might want to give him a call yourself. Remember, I'm the food and beverages gal… you do everything else. So this falls under *your* bailiwick, not mine!"

Tegan sighed heavily. "I'm just picking up the kids now. They're all going to be at my house doing their homework until you come to get Chelsea and Jake, so I'm not sure if I'll get a chance to call him until later."

"That will probably be okay. Do you have his number at home?"

"Yes, I've got it in his file. I've got the room reserved; the bar

1

setup is just like he wanted. I'll pick up the decorations tomorrow while the kids are at school, but this? I wonder if he plans on paying extra, or if he expects us to pay for a bimbo out of what he's paying us?"

Patti sighed. "You'd better negotiate with him on that. The appetizers alone that he wanted are running up his tab. You said he agreed to pay for the bar bill separately, but the ingredients for some of the foods have gone up a lot in the past couple of weeks. I was able to pre-order some of it, but some I just have to bite the bullet and pay whatever it costs, since it's fresh produce and I can't buy it ahead of time."

Tegan slowed down as she was approaching the school zone. "I'm beginning to regret having agreed to do this party. I was afraid we might be out of our league, running an all-men party, but he was willing to pay the price I quoted him, and he *is* Juanita's brother-in-law. I guess I'll have to see what I can do when I call him. Oops, there are the kids. See you later."

"I'll be over as soon as I can, but I'm getting the recipes for the food together and that may take awhile. Plan on about six, okay? But don't feed them dinner; I'll take care of that. Bye."

Tegan beeped the horn to get the attention of the four kids she was there to pick up. Two were hers, and two were Patti's. The two girls were eleven and in sixth grade, and they walked over from the nearby middle school to wait with their brothers to be picked up. The two boys were eight and in third grade. They had all known each other since they were babies, as their moms had been in the same playgroup, along with Juanita, and some of the other moms in their subdivision.

They had all been one big happy family way back then. That was before the divorces started, and the moms who were left alone had to rebuild their lives and make different plans for taking care of their kids.

The chatter of the kids now filled the car, and Tegan smiled as it all washed over her once again. She and Patti traded off, with one of them continuing to work at home on their business and one of them picking up the kids each day after school. While she usually enjoyed the business that she and her best friend had started almost two years ago, she also really liked pretending, on the days that she got to pick up the kids, that she was a stay-at-home mom again. So she settled down to just living in the moment, trying to concentrate on the conversations in the back and listening to the energy and enthusiasm of children newly freed from school.

As she had expected, they were all starving when they got to her house, and even though they knew that *she* wasn't the gourmet mom, they knew she would have something for them to eat, since feeding all four of them had been a part of her life as long as they had. The time flew by as she asked about their day, fed them snacks, liberally dispensed hugs and settled them all down to their homework. Katie and Chelsea complained about how much homework sixth-graders got, and she commiserated with them but reminded them that middle school was getting them ready for high school, so along with having multiple teachers for their classes, they were bound to have more work to do.

Since the girls had taken over the dining room table, the boys went upstairs to Kevin's room. After a time, using her well-honed mom instincts, Tegan snuck up to find them engrossed in the latest computer game that Kevin's dad had given to him for his birthday. After some arguments and discussion about earned rewards and how homework *had* to come first, the boys got their math books out and got to work.

Tegan then grabbed the opportunity to throw another load of

laundry into the washing machine, and got out a frozen casserole she had taken out to thaw earlier in the day. She put it into the oven, then snuck into her office to look for the file on the upcoming party. She had just found the file and begun to look for the client's phone number, when Katie yelled out, "Mom, you have to come here. You have to sign something."

A quick glance at her watch told her that it was already five-thirty. Patti would be by to pick up her kids soon. She told herself she'd take care of business after dinner and she went out to do her mom-duties again.

Two

Dinner involved the usual arguing over who needed to do what afterwards and the dishes ended up getting done after much negotiating and trading off kitchen duties. Then Katie took over the living room TV, and Kevin retreated up to his room to return to the new computer game. Figuring she might need a little extra control over her nerves, Tegan poured herself a glass of red wine... "For medicinal purposes, for my heart," she reminded herself, then went into her office and looked up the phone number she needed to call.

The phone was picked up on the first ring.

"Hello," said a low masculine voice belonging to Alexander Reyes, her current client.

"Hi, Mr. Reyes, this is Tegan O'Neill from Parties by Pat-Teg. Patti told me you called earlier today with a major change to the plans for your party next weekend. What can we do for you?"

There was a slight pause. "Didn't your partner tell you what I asked for? What is there to discuss?" He sounded impatient. He had picked up the phone on the first ring, so she imagined him sitting in a home office, as she was, and she took a sip of her wine.

"Well, Mr. Reyes, it's not like hiring a stripper is something I do every day. I'm not really sure how to begin to go about this. I don't personally *know* any strippers, and while I'm sure there are companies that supply them, I think this is really out of my jurisdiction. Can't you hire one yourself?"

"That is out of the question. I'm a very busy man… that's why I hired your company in the first place, to plan this party for me. The birthday guest of honor is a very important client, whose account I almost have guaranteed. This party is going to be the final way I can show him that I can supply anything he needs. I was told by my brother Edgar's wife you're very good at planning and implementing all of the details to make a memorable event run smoothly. I'm paying you a lot of money to provide everything I ask for, and the entertainment should be included in the package."

"Yes," Tegan took another sip of wine. "But the usual entertainment I have set up has included DJ's for music, or a live band, or clowns or magicians. I'm not even sure how to go about finding a stripper, much less making arrangements for an appearance. Should I look in the phone book, then call 'Strippers R Us'?"

"Tegan, listen closely to me." Alexander sounded as if he was talking to a child, "This is a very important client, whose account will bring a lot of money into my company; I have spent weeks trying to convince him to sign with me. In talking to my potential client, I recently discovered that he has never been to a strip club. Imagine that! Turning thirty and never even been to a bachelor party!"

"Imagine that," Tegan said dryly, taking another sip of wine. "Who knew?"

"Do you have some kind of problem with strip clubs, or strippers in general?" Alexander asked, sounding less bored and more amused.

"Well, I can't speak for *all* women, of course, but personally, I haven't ever been to a strip club and I can die happy even if I never set foot in one. I have never been able to understand the fascination of

6

looking at something you can't touch, but then, I've never been much into window-shopping either."

There was a snort of laughter from the phone. "Do you mean to tell me you don't like to look at attractive men, Ms. O'Neill?"

"Honey, I'm divorced. Looking is all I ever get to do anymore!" Tegan realized how desperate that sounded, so she hastily added, "Not that I'm complaining, of course. I have my business and my children to keep me busy."

She cleared her throat, thinking maybe the wine hadn't been such a good idea after all. "So, Mr. Reyes, to get back to business... I'll see what I can do to take care of your request before next Friday."

She swore she could hear him smiling into the phone. "Very well, Tegan. And please, call me Alex. I have the utmost confidence you will ensure my party is a complete success. And if I land the client's account, I might even consider a bonus as a way of thanking you for your contribution."

"Thanks, Alex. I guess I should look at it as learning on-the-job how to expand my repertoire of services I can provide to my customers, huh?"

"Then we have an understanding. Now I have two calls coming in on my other lines. Unless I hear from you, I will assume everything is taken care of, and I will see you a week from Friday at the party."

"Fine. See you then." Tegan hung up and swore at the phone. "What the hell? A stripper? Now I'm a pimp, too? Bite me, Mr. Reyes!"

She turned on her computer and went online. The pop-up ads started like crazy, once she began to look for companies that provided strippers. An hour later, after being assaulted with the close-up pictures of more surgically-enhanced breasts than she had ever wanted to see, some of which looked like they seriously threatened the women's ability to even stand upright, Tegan turned off her computer, went into the kitchen and got another glass of wine. Then she went back into her office and called Patti to complain about their latest client's unreasonable request.

Three

Alexander didn't get another chance to think about the party arrangements, or his talk with Tegan, until well after midnight when his business calls finally stopped. He sat back and rubbed his temples and smiled, amused at the memory of the soccer-mom called Tegan O'Neill, who had presented her contract to him in his office two weeks ago. He had called her on the advice of his brother, whose wife had been in something called a playgroup with her. Since he had no children, his first thought was of a group of naked women, including his sister-in-law, touching each other all over, with scented massage oils involved. He had broken out in a sweat and realized he had not taken enough time off work lately if he was so easily aroused.

He had been divorced for the past fourteen years. It was still fun to be free to pick up any interesting women he might meet. Most women still found him to be attractive, even though he was forty-two and starting to grey slightly. But it took time to find them, and time was something he was very short on.

The sales company he worked for was a very cut-throat business. He was paid on a commissions-only basis, and he thrived on the competition; in fact, he had earned himself the nickname "Sting-Reyes" for the deep sea predator he reminded his coworkers of. But sometimes he wished for some time off, or a reason to relax. Chasing women was a way to take his mind off his job, and he did enjoy the challenge of the pursuit; but dealing with losing them afterwards, always took more time than he wanted to give.

There was always the possibility they would have "rug-rats" back home they would neglect to tell him about, as if they were embarrassed to have them. Then they would want him to meet them, and expect him to step right into the role of surrogate dad, which was not something with which he had any experience. He didn't have anything against children, per se, but having grown up as the oldest in a family of nine, with both sets of grandparents living with them for most of his childhood, he had decided at an early age *not* ever to allow himself to be put into the situation of having a houseful of mouths to feed, and not enough money to do it.

He got himself a beer out of the fridge in his office and settled back into his chair, his feet on his desk. Maria, his ex-wife, had wanted children right after they got married. Her family lived in the same neighborhood as his, and they had started dating soon after she graduated from high school and he got out of college. Even back then, he was spending all of his time working. The idea of being married, and not having to go looking for sex to reduce his stress, had been the main reason he had gotten married. That, and Maria had been a wild woman in bed, willing to try anything he wanted, and good at it all. Damn! He was getting hard just thinking about her. But she was Hispanic like him, and had wanted to start a family when they were young and dirt-poor. He was not about to step into the same trap that had ensnared his father.

The divorce had been hard on both their families, but Alex had been offered a transfer out of state at just the right time, and he jumped at the chance to put some distance between him and his ex-wife, as well as his family. He now lived in the same state again, but he lived in downtown Chicago, far away from the neighborhood in Aurora where he had grown up. His mother often reminded him, when he called her, about how many children Maria had with her second husband and how happy they were. But he had seen her at a local grocery store on one of his last visits home. She was plump and round with another pregnancy and surrounded by small children who were making demands on her. She had looked harried and stressed, but was happy to say hello to an old friend, as she told the children he was. He had felt inordinately grateful he had escaped when he had, and left her to happily pursue repeated motherhood with a more malleable man than he.

So now, he thought back to his earlier conversation of the evening. Why had he been thinking about Maria again? Oh yeah, sex. Not enough of it in his life these days. He knew at some point, his libido was supposed to be slowing down, but some days he felt like a horny, hormonal teenager again. Especially when it had been so long since he had been with a woman.

And what had made him think about sex? The phone call from the party planner he had hired, to make sure he got the new client he had been pursuing. He smiled thinking how uncomfortable she appeared to be with his simple request for a stripper. This was the twenty-first century, damn it! What was the big deal? *Playboy* magazine had celebrated its fiftieth year in business recently. No one thought anything of it when men held business meetings in strip clubs. Sure, the women on the sales team were not real happy about it, but too bad! If you want to succeed in a man's world, doing a man's job, you have to learn to be tough.

Then he thought about the conservatively-dressed woman who had sat across from him in his office weeks ago, earnestly explaining the

11

contract she wanted him to sign. She had listed all of the services she and her partner were to provide for him at the party, and once he heard the word services, all he could think about was pulling her across his desk and having her service him right then and there. Shit! It *really* had been too long for him this time. He was going to have to give himself permission to have some vacation time really soon, before he started assaulting random women in the streets.

He concentrated on remembering what Ms. Tegan O'Neill looked like while she leaned across his desk to point out things in the contract, just a hint of cleavage exposed. She was really Irish, and not just by marriage, of that much he was sure. Her pale skin had freckles sprinkled across her face, and her short, light brown hair had a red tint to it that probably came from a bottle, but suited her well. He guessed her to be close to him in age, and that was a big negative for him. As a single man, he liked to take his pick of the twenty-somethings who congregated in the watering holes salesmen like to frequent after work. While they were usually too thin for his taste, and he had very little in common with them to talk about, at least they were willing to try new things in bed, and most were happy with one-night stands. Women his age were looking to get married, and "been there, done that, never again," had become his slogan.

When they had both stood up to shake hands on the closed deal, he noticed she was tall for a woman; he estimated she was only a few inches shorter than his six-feet. But on her way out of the office, he had admired her nicely shaped rear in her baggy clothes. She was definitely an interesting woman, but she was someone he was doing business with now, and he always kept to his rule about not mixing business with pleasure. So no matter how cute her face looked when it dimpled as she smiled, he was not going to act on his attraction. At least not with her.

Later, in the shower, he thought about moments spent with Maria when they were both still young, and was surprised when, at the moment of giving himself up to pleasure, the face and body of the Irish woman imposed itself in his mind. It was in the fantasy of her that he found his release.

Four

Tegan and Patti were sitting in Patti's dining room a week later working on the final details of the upcoming party for Alexander Reyes. It was after dinner and their kids were all in the family room downstairs fighting over the TV and video games, so they were trying to get some work done. Patti had done a wonderful job of acquiring all of the recipes and ingredients for the appetizers and tapas that were requested, but all Tegan could think of was that she had been unable to find him a stripper.

Some of the people at the agencies she had called had laughed at her, pointing out they booked their girls months in advance, so there was no one available on such short notice. She had nastily countered by asking them if those girls were over eighteen... if not, selling them nude was against the law. If so, they weren't girls anymore. More than one had hung up on her.

A couple of the agencies were willing to work with her, to get her a stripper for the night in question, but there would be a huge finder's fee to make up for the short notice, in addition to their regular charges. This meant there wouldn't be much profit left at all for Parties by Pat-Teg after all the bills had been paid. Since both she and Patti had bills of their own to pay, and the child support and alimony only went so far, this was not a good choice.

What had really surprised Tegan was how detailed the questions were that the agencies asked her. Since she had no idea how to answer them, she had written the questions down, meaning to ask her client exactly *what* kind of stripper he had in mind. Now she shared some of these questions with Patti, as they worked on the bottle of wine they had opened over dinner.

"So, what kind of questions do they ask?" Patti had opened the topic for discussion.

"Well, they first want to know just how little the dancers are expected to strip down to... you know, can nipples be covered, or do they have to be seen? Do the panties stay on, or do they come off? If they are removed, is hair allowed, or does it have to be shaved? Are they expected to touch themselves, or to let anyone else touch them? Is anyone, including the guest of honor, going to want a lap dance?"

"Boy, oh boy, who knew there was so much involved with taking your clothes off so men could drool on themselves looking at you?" mused Patti.

"Then they also want to know if there's a theme requested." At the puzzled look on Patti's face, she continued. "You know: western gal, stewardess, nurse, harem girl, French maid, British school-girl..." she stopped because they had both started giggling.

"How about All-American cheerleader?" Patti asked.

"Or drug-addicted, anorexic super-model?" Tegan giggled even more.

"Or just that old favorite, skanky whore?" Patti suggested with a snort.

At this they both laughed heartily, then poured themselves more wine.

"One thing is for sure... they don't want ordinary housewives in sweat pants and torn cotton panties, huh?" Tegan gasped, wiping the tears from her eyes.

"I'll bet they wouldn't turn down 'Desperate Housewives' though!" Patti said, hiccupping from laughter. They both continued to laugh for a few minutes.

"Well, we're pretty 'desperate,' aren't we?" Tegan turned serious. "I don't know about you, but I really need my half of the full amount of money we are going to make off of this party. Katie's going to need braces soon, and Kevin broke his bike last week. I had to tell him we couldn't afford a new one, but I hate for him not to have a bike to ride around the neighborhood, since he spends too much time in his room on those damn computer games the way it is!"

There was a silence, as both of them mused over their finances, which was always a downer.

Patti broke the quiet. "Then why don't *you* do it?"

"Do what?"

"Why don't *you* strip for the party?"

"Are you out of your fucking mind?" Tegan shrieked, then lowered her voice when the sound of the children fighting downstairs ended. "What are you, crazy?" she hissed.

"Well, not really, "said Patti, suddenly all business. "Obviously I can't do it for two main reasons. One, I'm the food person, so I have to be there to do the cooking and the supervising of the serving of the food. And two, I don't really think that lard-ass, as my ex so fondly used to call me, is one of the most-requested themes for strippers!"

Tegan opened her mouth to protest, but they were old friends and often knew what the other was going to say before it was said.

"No, really, I know I'm too fat for most guys to find sexy, as Jake used to tell me all of the time. But tough shit... I can cook and bake circles around all of the skinny gals, who need silicone in their boobs to make them big. These are all-natural, baby!" She smiled.

16

Tegan looked thoughtful. "Do you really think I have the body to be a stripper? I mean, just for the one night?"

"Honey, I've seen guys watching you in public, like at the grocery store. Yeah, I think they'd pay to see you strip naked for them.

"I'm *not* stripping all the way naked for anyone!"

"Isn't that one of the questions you said they asked? If full nudity was required or if g-strings were allowed to stay on?"

"Yes. I suppose I *could* tell him no one would do full nudity on such short notice, but I *was* able to find a dancer willing to go *most* of the way."

"Have some more wine," Patti said, as she poured the last of the bottle into their glasses.

"God, I don't know if I have the guts to be half-naked in front of a room full of men! I haven't even dressed sleazy since John stopped finding me attractive... or at least since he *told* me he didn't find me sexy at all."

"See, that's why it's such a good idea for you!" Patti said excitedly. "Your confidence was shot to hell when John told you he was gay and leaving you for a man! Maybe having a bunch of slightly drunk younger guys getting all horny over you will make you realize that there's nothing wrong with you! It was *his* fault and not *yours* that you stopped having a sex life."

"Yeah, but I'm going to be forty next year. I've had two children by c-section. I have stretch marks and surgical scars that are never going away!"

"And you still wear a size ten, girl! You still turn heads wherever you go. And you are *really* hot in a bathing suit! Shit, if I looked like you, I'd go braless everywhere and screw everyone from the mailman to the college student bagboys at the grocery store!"

They both laughed, since everyone in the neighborhood had the hots for their good-looking young mailman, whose unseen physical attributes had been a source of much speculation for years at playgroup meetings.

"I don't know how to strip dance, though. What about that?" Tegan asked.

"How hard can it be to take your clothes off to music?" Patti snorted. "Hey, rent that movie from a few years back that had that blond actress in it, where she becomes a stripper. I'll bet after watching that a couple of times, you'll be able to bump-and-grind along with the best of them!"

"Well, we *have* been doing some pole-dancing kind of movements in my Jazzercise classes lately. Some real hip-rolling stuff that a lot of the women can't do, but I can!"

"That's the spirit!" said Patti, "And I'll bet you still have some lingerie lying around that might not have done much for Mr. 'Honey, I'm gay,' but would probably blow the minds of a bunch of thirty-year olds who haven't ever been to a strip club."

"Do you really think I can pull this off, or are we just too drunk to know any better?" Tegan finally asked, after taking a moment to think it over.

"Probably a little of both," Patti admitted. "But if it will make you feel better, I'll be sure to have a bottle of wine for you at the party, so when you get there to change into your dancing shoes, you'll be able to get yourself in the mood. And look at it this way... it will only be a few minutes of dancing, a few minutes of semi-nudity, then you can head out the door, grab your clothes from the room you changed in and leave. I can take care of the party myself, and you'll never have to see any of those guys again, so who cares? The only one who might recognize you is Alexander, but you only met him once, right? And since he's the one who's insisting on a stripper, you can always tell him afterwards there weren't any available, and since we are full-service party-planners, we didn't want to disappoint him."

"I feel so wicked! 'Ordinary housewife/businesswoman and mom by day, stripper by night!' What a double life! Maybe I'll like it so much, I can make that my night job and we can add a whole new list of services that Parties by Pat-Teg can supply!"

With that, they both giggled some more, then had to pull themselves together when Katie came in and asked in an aggrieved tone when they were going home. "After all, Mom, it *is* a school night!"

Later that night after the kids were in bed, Tegan pulled a suitcase out of the back of her closet, and used the key to open it. There were silk lingerie, garter belts, some g-strings, even some bra tops that barely covered her nipples. As always, just trying it on made her horny and she sighed with frustration, knowing she was going to have to pleasure herself, since no one else seemed to want to. Deciding she could put together the whole costume, layer by layer, tomorrow when the kids were in school, she took a long shower, then slipped into bed with "Mr. Happy," who was always in the mood to please her, as long as the batteries worked.

Five

Putting a costume together, or rather, three layers of costume, didn't really prove to be that difficult. Tegan had gone to a lot of trouble to entice her husband into bed back in the days when he could still be talked into it. She had wondered why his libido had taken such a nosedive after the birth of their second child, so she had worked out and dieted like crazy in order to get back, as closely as possible, to her pre-pregnancy weight. Then she had gone on binges of buying lingerie, and done everything she could think of, because her sex drive had come back with a vengeance after Kevin stopped nursing. John had actually bought "Mr. Happy" for her birthday one year, telling her, "He can take my place when I'm just too damn tired from working all day to support my family."

When the weeks in between love making stretched into months and then years, she knew something was seriously wrong with their marriage. Still, nothing could have prepared her for the shock of having her husband of fifteen years tell her he was leaving her for a man. He told her he never meant to hurt her, and he had been denying what he was even to himself, for years. But he had met someone special, and they were tired of sneaking around to see each other.

She wasn't sure if she was more hurt by the fact he had been cheating on her, or by the fact he was having sex and she wasn't. But the fact he no longer found her attractive in any way, was devastating to her self-esteem.

As she sobbed on Patti's shoulder, she told her, "At least if it was another woman, I would know how to fight! I'm better in bed than most women I know. I've worked harder at it, and enjoy it more than most do. Before I met John, I had other lovers tell me if they ever wanted to settle down with just one woman, they would want someone like me, someone who was always willing to try new positions and who always enjoyed herself as much, if not more, than they did."

And Patti, who had gone through her own messy divorce the previous year, when she had caught her philandering husband "in the act" with his secretary in the closet at the office Christmas party, had held her and said, "There, there," and commiserated with her over enough bottles of wine, so that eventually the pain subsided into an ever-present, but no-longer-throbbing ache. There were no single men in their subdivision, and both of them swore they would cut off their own arms first before they would have an affair with a married man. Having been on the receiving end of the discovery and aftermath of being the neglected spouse, they were not about to inflict that kind of pain on any other woman.

Since finding a new man appeared to be difficult, if not impossible, while raising their children, they decided to go into business together. Child support and alimony only went so far in paying their bills, so this was part of the reason they became small-businesswomen. But the other reason was they both had a huge void in their lives that used to be filled with a relationship with a husband; even when it was a strained relationship, it still took up a lot of time. And now that both of their children were in school all day, they took inventory of their mutual strengths and decided on opening an event-planning business.

For years, Patti had been working on her gourmet cooking skills. As her ex-husband used to tell everyone who ate at their house, "One thing my wife knows is how to make good food. You can tell, since she eats so much of it herself."

Since he was not the thinnest man on the block, Tegan used to roll her eyes at Patti and mimic rubbing a huge belly. Truly, they had gotten each other through some really rough times, and in the time-honored way of close women-friends, they depended on each other even more than if they had been blood sisters.

As Patti was to satisfying taste buds, so was Tegan to organizing things. She joked her parents must have potty-trained her as an infant, since she was anal-retentive to the max. She liked nothing better than to walk into a mess and impose order on it. For years, she had been the one to plan all of the playgroup outings, and be the room mother for her children's classrooms.

When they took inventory of their skills, asking themselves how they could possibly supplement their incomes by working out of their homes, the only viable option they could see was to do event planning, or party planning. They had come up with a name for their business, and gotten a small-business loan to print up business cards and letterhead. Then they had printed up flyers and put them wherever they knew mothers congregated with their children. They had gotten only sporadic calls for the first few months, but as they had more successful parties under their belts, their reputation grew by word-of-mouth. Now they found they were able to keep busy year-round. Holidays might be a big part of their business, but so were birthdays, which happened all year.

When Alexander Reyes had first called about using their company for a party he needed to throw, Tegan had had reservations about it because they had never done a party for men-only before. They had done many children's birthday parties and women-only events, like

22

wedding and baby showers; they had even done mixed-couples events, like holiday parties. Planning a party for just men seemed to be a bit more difficult. But Alexander was insistent, since as he told her on the phone, he was a very busy man and had no time to shop around for a party planning service. His sister-in-law told him she had used their company a couple of times, and he had been at her last Christmas party, and been impressed by the canapés and the champagne punch. So he wanted them to help him land an important client, and he was willing to pay whatever charge she would name.

He gave her a list of foods he wanted served, heavy on the Mexican spices and flavors that were Patti's favorite to work with, since she liked eating hot foods so much. And he requested a place with an open bar, and said he would pay that tab separately. Despite their reservations, Tegan and Patti had accepted the job, and now Tegan found herself standing in front of her mirror, blasting music she had downloaded off I-Tunes, trying to make up a routine that would allow her to slowly remove her clothing, while gyrating her hips and shaking her booty.

She had to admit to herself, though reluctantly, she looked pretty good in each of the layers of costume she had put together. She figured out the key to *not* feeling ridiculous was to imagine she was moving her body to get the man she most wanted so hot he would want to throw her over his shoulder and hustle her off to his bed as soon as she was done dancing. Even more reluctantly, she admitted to herself that watching herself dance, in fact, just doing the dancing, was making her hornier than she had felt in years, and that was really unnerving!

She remembered all of the agencies telling her, when she complained about their high prices, that part of the bill included the bodyguard that would accompany the dancers to the party. She wondered if that was to protect the strippers from their audience, or to stop the dancers from over-stepping their bounds and jumping on the men who were watching them. She imagined how hard all of the men would be getting when she moved her hips like this, and like that, and realized she would have to leave right after her act, and not only because she would be too embarrassed to look at any of them in the face afterwards. If this was how she was reacting to just imagining how they would look when they watched her, after her actual performance she was going to have to rush back home for a long, cold shower, then a hot date with Mr. Happy!

"Nope," she said to her reflection in the mirror. "I'm not going to start doing this as a second job anytime in the near future! At least not when I still have young kids at home who would be mortified to find out what a wanton hussy their mother is!"

She rehearsed her routine a few more times until it was time to change back into her mom clothes and go pick up the kids from school. She carefully packed her outfits and her music into a duffel bag, put Katie's boom box on top of it and prayed for the confidence to be able to pull this off, just this once, tomorrow night. Then she put it in her closet and went off to add her small car to the line of mini-vans at the school.

Six

Thursday night had been curriculum night for third grade. After school, Tegan had picked up the kids and fed them all dinner so Patti could do some of the cooking for tomorrow night's party. Then they had Juanita's oldest daughter, Rosa, come over to do her homework with the kids so there would be a teenager in the house. She was also going to be over Friday night; even though she was only fourteen, she had been babysitting her own siblings for years. That, and the fact her parents would be home and lived only a few houses down from Tegan, made her an ideal choice when both moms had to be out running parties.

Since Kevin and Jake Jr. were not in the same class, Tegan and Patti had barely seen each other during curriculum night. But they walked out the door to the parking lot together, and Patti waited until they were in her car to ask. "So, are you ready for tomorrow night?"

Tegan groaned and rolled her eyes. "As ready as I'll ever be, I guess. Sometimes I wonder how I let myself get into these things! At this point, I'm figuring even though I won't be that sexy, the men will be so busy laughing at my clumsy attempts to turn them on, they will have a good time, regardless of my lack of dancing skills."

25

"That's the spirit. Keep 'em laughing and coming back for more." Patti smiled at her, as they got to her house and got out of the car so Patti could get her kids.

"No! Coming back for more food, fine; more alcohol, fine. But once I leave the room after the dance, I'm out of there. I'll be too embarrassed even to look at myself in the eyes in the mirror for a while. Never mind the wine ahead of time. I'm going to need a gallon of it when I get back home."

They both giggled. "Don't tell Rosa you are planning on getting drunk, though. You know how people in this subdivision talk about each other. Our business reputation will be trashed if they think we eat...well, they know I do, and drink... okay, both of us do, what we provide."

"And we certainly don't want them finding out about our mystery stripper, since they'll want one at all of their future retirement parties and bar mitzvahs!"

"Yeah, that'll make their rabbis' long straight hair curl, huh?"

They both waited a moment, laughing on the front porch, until they were composed enough to go in the door.

Later, with the kids in bed, Tegan thought about practicing the routine once again, but she had spent the better part of the afternoon making sure she knew exactly what she was going to do and when, so she gave herself a pedicure, took a long, hot bath, then got into bed with Mr. Happy, but she fell asleep too quickly to take advantage of his ability to please her.

Seven

Alexander took another bite of the *chili rellenos* on his plate and looked around with great satisfaction. The evening was turning out to be a major success. The guest of honor was having such a great time that he had already pulled Alexander aside and confided in a slightly slurred voice that he was going to formally give his account to him Monday morning, but in actuality, it was already his. His friends were all daring him to do shots now to celebrate his thirtieth birthday, and all of the appetizers and tapas were proclaimed to be "the best." The only thing missing was the entertainment Tegan had assured him would be arriving at ten, and it was now five minutes past.

Alexander was a patient man, but he walked over to the food table and asked, "So, Patti, where is your partner this evening? She had told me she'd see me here, but I'm not seeing her. And speaking of *not* seeing, where is the entertainment? Or was she unable to fulfill my request, so she's ashamed to show her face here?"

A slow smile spread across Patti's face as she said, "Why, Mr. Reyes, the entertainment's just arrived. See for yourself." She gestured behind him and Alexander turned around to see a woman in a trench coat and oversized hat, along with very dark sunglasses, stride into the room and plug in a boom box in the outlet by the door.

27

She had long blonde hair and stilettos with four-inch heels, so she was an imposing figure at over six feet tall.

Once the music started, the men doing shots at the bar noticed her and a shocked silence fell over them as they watched her slowly dance her way over to the center of the room. Once there, she unbuttoned her trench coat and tossed her hat back towards the door. In time to the slow, sensuous beat of the bluesy-style music, she slowly removed her coat to reveal a white silky blouse buttoned all the way up, but thin enough for her black bra to be seen through it, barely containing her ample breasts with their hard, pointy nipples poking through the fabric and demanding attention.

Alexander's mouth went dry and he could barely swallow. The other men were moving closer, grabbing chairs to sit on... settling down to watch, fascinated, as the woman tossed the coat back to join the hat. They saw a black leather skirt, short enough for the black garters holding up the black silk stockings, to be seen. The music changed to the Santana song, "Black Magic Woman," which had always been one of Alexander's favorite's to use to seduce women, since he had learned to do the cha-cha before he had even learned to walk.

Obviously this woman had learned from a master, since her dancing was flawlessly executed, and it was all Alexander could do to keep himself standing in one place and not rushing over to do the dance of love with her. As she danced, she swayed her hips and used her hands to draw attention alternately to her hips, then to the buttons on her blouse that she was slowly unbuttoning, one at a time from the top down. Once she got all of the buttons undone, she teased them all by pretending to remove her blouse, flashing them with a quick view of her breasts spilling over the bra, then she put it back on to dance around some more.

By this time, the other men were making noises of excitement and enjoyment, as men usually do when they are in a group, and getting turned on together by a scene they can't join, but can enjoy watching. No one attempted to touch her; they seemed to know all they could do was watch. Alexander found himself unable to move even if he had wanted to, since his erection had grown so large his pants were too tight for him to even sit down.

The woman tossed off her blouse to join the hat and coat and began to sway her hips as she worked her hands around her abdomen, fondling herself, until she got both hands to the back of the skirt and drew down the zipper. This movement made her breasts almost fall out of the front of the bra and the catcalls reflected the excitement the audience was feeling as they waited hopefully for her naked breasts to make an appearance. The bra held its cargo in position, and the skirt was slowly drawn down, inch by inch, to reveal a black lacy thong that matched the bra. The dancer slowly stepped out of the skirt and that was thrown over to join the other discarded clothing.

Beads of sweat were now on Alexander's face and he could feel them trickle down under his shirt and run down his legs. He didn't think it was possible for him to feel any more aroused than he already was, when the music changed again, and this time to an Arabic-sounding piece of music that made the woman begin to belly dance and bump and grind her hips as if she was doing a world-class pole dance, only without a pole to rub herself on.

Her breasts rose and fell with her heavy breathing; her rounded abdomen and hips begged for someone to grab them and pleasure her, and the stockings and garters only served to emphasize the long legs she was using to dance around the middle of the room. The thong left little to the imagination, and Alexander suddenly felt as if the room didn't hold enough oxygen for him to breathe. Not being able to move, or take his eyes off of the blonde temptress he had paid for, he raised his eyes to look away from the killer body that threatened to make him embarrass himself by coming in his pants in front of men with whom he couldn't afford such a gaffe.

The fact they all seemed to be feeling the same way didn't matter. He was the senior man here, the alpha. He was the host and the only one who had been to strip clubs before. What shocked him the most was this woman didn't have the bored look most of the strippers he had seen wore when they were dancing. She actually seemed to be as turned on by her dancing, as the men who were watching her were, and for that reason alone, she was worth every penny she was being paid. He shook his head, trying to clear it, as he studied her face. The dark glasses were still on, but she had a dreamy, aroused look on her face. Then she smiled in response to a hooted invitation from one of the men, and Alexander almost swallowed his own tongue as he recognized her dimples.

Eight

Tegan was lost in the music, enjoying the fact that whenever she moved, the men appreciated it and shouted out their encouragement. They were inviting her to "Take it off, take it all off!" She shook her head each time they yelled that at her, but she was sorely tempted to at least rip off her bra and let them see how hot an almost-forty-year old woman could be. She slowly circled around, letting everyone in the room get a good view of her from all sides, and found herself looking directly into the smoldering eyes of the man who was responsible for her being here. Their eyes locked and she found it impossible to look away.

She remembered she had decided to dance as if she was trying to make the man she most wanted so hot he wouldn't be able to resist her. The shock of recognition was on his face, along with a passion deep enough for her to want to drown herself in it. She slowly undulated towards him, inviting him with her arms to join her. His eyes were almost black with arousal, and he looked dazed as he slowly began to move forward.

At that moment, she caught sight of Patti standing behind him, with her hands on her hips and a look of warning on her face, as she slowly shook her head, mouthing, "*No!* Don't do it!"

31

This acted like a slap of cold water in Tegan's face, as she realized she was about ten seconds away from throwing herself on her client, having real sex with him in the middle of his party and he was ready to go along with her!

The music changed again, and she used the blues music as a coda to her dancing, as she slowly backed away from the center of the room, still swaying her hips but retreating back to where her clothes were, along with the boom box, by the door. Keeping her back to the door, she bent over, grabbed all of her discarded clothing, ripped the plug out of the wall and made a hasty exit into the hallway.

She almost ran, as best she could in four-inch heels, down the hall to the manager's office, where she had been allowed to change into her dancing clothes. There wasn't anyone in the office, and her other clothes were where she had left them on a couch in the waiting room outside the manager's inner office. By the light coming in from the door open to the hallway, she saw the desk where a secretary sat during the day. She threw the boom box and the sunglasses down on the desktop and turned on a small light, then turned to go back to close the door so she could change her clothes. She kicked off her shoes as she turned around, then froze.

Alexander stood in the doorway, and whether it was a trick of the light or the apprehension she immediately felt, he seemed to take up all of the door space and block the light. He wordlessly entered the room and closed the door behind him. Then he turned and in a few quick long strides, he was directly in front of her. She realized she was shaking, and not from the cold. Heat radiated from him to her, and she was unable to move or speak. He raised his hand to brush her wig's long blonde hair back from her shoulder, and she saw his hand was shaking as well.

He raised that hand and gently placed it under her chin, and lifted her face to look directly into his eyes. Passion had darkened them so

32

much there was no color visible in them anymore. He lowered his head and brushed his lips gently against hers; it felt like a question, and she wasn't sure how to respond. She stopped breathing for a heartbeat. Then sweat broke out all over her body and she surrendered to what she most wanted to do at that moment: she pressed herself against the length of his body and wrapped her arms around his back, up and under his shirt, to feel the hard muscles coiled under the skin of his shoulders and back. She tore open the buttons as her hands circled around to the front of him; his dark body hair inflamed her, making her rub her face on it and lick at his muscular chest.

With a low groan, he took her wordless surrender for what it was, and his hands moved over her body as he traced her curves, setting her on fire wherever he touched, pulling her close and pressing her against his insistent erection. His lips were busy kissing and licking his way across her face to her neck, to her ear, then her shoulder, as he expertly undid her bra with one hand. He used the other hand to slide the strap off one side, then the other, setting her breasts free for him to see. But seeing wasn't enough for him, and he lowered his head to lick and kiss each breast in turn, massaging them gently, then holding them up so his waiting lips could suckle each nipple in turn, while twisting and pulling on the other one with his other hand.

Tegan lost what little control she had over herself, wanting only one thing: this man inside of her body. She frantically tore at his belt and got his pants undone, pushed the impossibly tight briefs down, then pulled his engorged organ out and almost fainted at the size of it. Holding a real penis in her hands again was a thrill in itself, but she wasn't going to be stopped from getting what she wanted from this man. And the man in question was just as anxious as she was to achieve the same goal.

Using one hand under her hips, he raised her up to rest her butt on the desk, which tilted her back just enough for him to be able to enter her, and enter her he did! Pushing her thong to the one side, he rolled the head of himself around, discovering that her dancing had made her so wet there was no need for any other foreplay. Then, with one massive push of his hips, he shoved himself into her until she felt his balls dangle on her butt. Just the feel of him in her made her spiral into an orgasm that caught them both by surprise. She dug her fingers into his back as she moaned, then trembled with the intensity of it. Then he began to move in and out of her, each time pulling almost all of the way out, then pushing his way back into her, making her tremble with repeated spasms each time he was flush against her body.

Her eyes were closed, but she opened them to watch the look of concentration on his face as he stimulated them both repeatedly, and she matched his movements, push for push, feeling her inner muscles tightening around him, as his strokes got faster and more frantic. The cords of muscle were standing out in his neck as he brought them both closer and closer to the edge of insanity, yet still he withdrew and entered, until his movements got shallower, as if he couldn't stand to be completely out of her anymore. With a mighty roar, he pushed one final time and she felt herself fall over the edge and scream on the way down, barely aware that his heat sprayed up into her with such force she expected to taste it.

They collapsed against each other, breathing ragged, pulses racing, holding each other up as their bodies kept them joined together. Slowly their pulses returned to normal and their breathing resumed independent patterns. Alexander was still semi-hard, as he reluctantly pulled himself out of her and leaned his forehead against hers for an instant, then gently stroked her face with both of his hands.

"Dios mío! Tegan, there's no excuse for what I just did to you. I'm so sorry!"

She shook her head, then moved her eyes up to look directly into his. "It's okay. I'm not sorry. But no one finds out about this and it can't happen again. Deal?"

Wordlessly he nodded, then she gave him a gentle shove, lowered herself off the desk and began to dress herself in the shorts and tee shirt she had arrived in. As she gathered up all of her costume and shoved it into the duffel bag, he pulled his pants up and gingerly zipped his pants over his still-eager organ. He buttoned up his shirt and watched as she walked over to the door. She turned to give him a small smile, but the look in her eyes was almost invitation enough for him to rush over to take her again. Then she opened the door and walked through it.

Nine

"What a fucking idiot I am!" he muttered to himself, looking around the room to be sure there wasn't any evidence of what had just occurred here. And what had just occurred? He had acted like an animal, driven mad by the fact it had been so damn long since he had been with a woman, and the come-and-get-me dancing the woman had been doing had driven him over the edge. He had totally lost control over himself, and once the thin veneer of civilization was torn off him, he had taken her without even asking her permission... taken her, and now could think of nothing else but wanting to take her again and again. He had promised himself to keep his hands off her, since they were doing business together, and now what?

Not only did he feel incapable of never touching her again, but he was sure she wanted him also. Her body had melted in his hands, in his mouth, like a piece of soft taffy that looked solid until the heat from your body melted it to allow the sweet taste of it to tantalize you into wanting more. He tried to be ashamed of himself, of their wordless encounter, but all he could think about was the other positions he wanted to have her in, the other ways he wanted to pleasure her; he wanted to hear her moan and scream for him again, and he had to figure out a way for that to happen.

Just then, his eyes lit upon some possible reasons for him to ask for a face-to-face meeting again. She had left her boom box and her sunglasses on the desk. She had been too rattled to remember them! He had to be right; she had to want him again also. And Alexander, who had not wanted to be with any woman more than once or twice in a very long time, wondered if he might finally have met his match. A wicked smile played around his lips, as he said aloud. "You don't think we should be together again, do you, Ms. O'Neill? Well, we'll see about that, won't we?"

He straightened up the desk, turned off the light, put the sunglasses into his pocket and picked up the boom box. He closed the door behind him and walked down the hall into the party room where his guests were still in high spirits and getting drunker by the minute. They greeted his reappearance with shouts, and teased him about where he could have been all of this time, asking him if he happened to pass the gorgeous stripper on his way down the hall. He laughed and said, "I wish," then sidled over to Patti, who was piling the dirty serving plates into her carrying cases.

He placed the boom box on a chair close to her and said, "I found this in the manager's office after your partner left the door open and headed out to the parking lot. Be sure to give her my thanks for her part in my party's success."

He smiled at her, at the surprised look on her face. "Of course the food was exceptional, but then, I knew it would be. I've tasted your cooking before. If you ever want to open a restaurant, I'd be willing to back you. Now I'd better get back to my guests and see which ones need a cab to get them home."

The rest of the evening was spent calling cabs and girlfriends or wives to come and pick up the men who weren't able to drive themselves home. Alexander drove three of them home himself, because his car only had room for three passengers, one of whom was his client, the birthday boy. It was much later before Alexander arrived back at his own place, and with a massive sigh of relief, he kicked off his shoes, grabbed a beer out of the kitchen fridge and threw himself backwards onto the closest couch. He pulled the sunglasses out of his pocket, and on a whim, lifted them to his nose. There was the unmistakable smell of the woman who had been wearing them: a mixture of her perfume and her sweat. Immediately he was rock-hard again, and he began to plot his strategy for getting her into his bed, where he could take his time giving them both pleasure beyond imagination. But then, when it came to sex, he had always had an overly-developed imagination. He smiled.

Ten

Tegan drove so fast going home she didn't have time to think about anything else except not getting a ticket. She knew a cop would have no idea what she had on under her shorts and tee shirt, but she didn't want to chance anyone finding out what a wanton woman she really was. When she got home, she found Rosa watching TV in the living room, and the kids all asleep upstairs. Since they frequently stayed over at each others' houses, this wasn't anything unusual. So she paid Rosa for the babysitting and sent her home, watching from her front porch until she saw Rosa enter her own front door.

She went upstairs to peek in on the kids and found the girls were indeed asleep, but the boys were still playing the computer games they loved. She told them to turn it off and get to sleep. They complained, but since both of them were yawning while they argued, she figured they'd turn in soon, and she left them to go fill her bathtub with water.

She was soaking in a bubble bath with a glass of wine in her hand and candles lit all around the room, when her cell phone rang. Since she was expecting the call; she had it on a chair next to the tub.

"Hello, Patti?"

"No, it's me," Alexander's low voice made her feel like her bones were melting. "Have dinner with me tomorrow night?"

"No! I can't get a sitter on such short notice!"

"The night after that?"

"*No!*"

"When?"

"Never! I told you, it's not going to happen again! Goodnight, Alex." She hung up the phone.

Alexander smiled at the phone in his hand. "Ah, but it *is* going to happen again. The only thing you can negotiate with me is where and when."

Then he took a long hot shower, and for the first time in a long time, didn't pleasure himself while he was under the steamy water.

"No," he mused, "I'm going to save it for her. And it will be sooner than she thinks."

He was still smiling when he fell asleep.

Eleven

When the phone rang a second time, Tegan almost let the voice mail get it, but figured that was the coward's way out.

"Hello?" She said tentatively.

"What the hell happened to you after your dance-act, Tegan?" Her best friend and partner yelled into the phone. "And how the hell did Alex get your boom box? What were you doing in the office that you forgot Katie's boom box in there? Well? What do you have to say for yourself?"

Tegan smiled. "Let's just say Alex expressed his appreciation for my dancing talents in a very physical way, and leave it at that, okay?"

There was a short silence, then, "Oh my God, Tegan! You bonked a client? In the manager's office?"

Tegan giggled.

"You go, girl!" Patti said, then she began singing, "She's 'back in the saddle again'!"

Tegan giggled. "Oh, stop! I told him it's never going to happen again."

"Bullshit! He's too hot for you for it not to happen again! I thought he was going to jump on you on the dance floor, in the middle of his important party!"

"Really?" Tegan asked.

"Yeah, you should have seen him watching you... I was ready to put a drool cup under his chin to keep his shirt dry!"

There was a moment of silence, then Patti said, "Well?"

"Well, what?"

"Well, how the hell was he? As hot as he looks?"

"Hotter! And bigger than you'd think!"

"Big, hot and Latino! You've hit a trifecta, girl! When are you going to see him again?"

"Like I just said, I told him it's not going to happen again. I can't take the risk of the kids finding out what a hussy their mom is."

"Bullshit again. There's no reason for you not to go on dates."

"But I don't think he wants to date... just to screw."

"That would be a problem, unless you only see him on John's weekends."

Tegan sighed. "Well, we'll have to see. For now, I'm just thrilled to have had a real penis in me again, since Mr. Happy has been kind of unsatisfying lately."

"Did he use a condom?"

"Who, Mr. Happy? He doesn't need one."

"Ha ha. I mean Mr. Hot Latino Lover."

"No, but my period is due tomorrow, and I'm like clockwork these days, remember? If I don't have it by midnight tomorrow, I might begin to be concerned. But for now, I'm just going to lie back in my tub and remember."

Patti sighed. "I'm so jealous I could spit. But also so happy for you that I'm going to keep my jealousy to myself, for now. So go ahead and soak in your tub. I'm going to go make myself a stiff drink, since that's the only thing that's stiff around here. The kids are asleep?"

"Yeah, the girls are. The boys were compu-gaming, but I told them to stop yawning and get to bed. It's been pretty quiet up there, so I think they listened to me. You coming to get them early?"

"No, I think we all need to sleep in tomorrow... *some* of us more than others."

Tegan giggled. "Then goodnight, partner. See you tomorrow."

Patti sighed. "Yeah, sweet dreams girl. See ya."

Tegan smiled as she hung up the phone. Maybe Patti was right... what harm was there in having an affair? As long as the kids didn't get attached to the guy, so they wouldn't have to be hurt by the eventual loss when he got tired of her, there wouldn't be a problem, right? She'd be hurt, but she had lived through much worse recently. And maybe this time she could keep her emotions in check and just enjoy the physical pleasure for what it was. She got out of the tub and dried herself off, then crawled into bed and was asleep before her head hit the pillow.

Alexander tried calling Tegan a couple of times over the weekend, but each time when a child answered the phone, he hung up without saying anything.

He sighed with frustration, saying out loud to his phone, "Okay, that's the way you want to play it, huh? Now let me think... how can I get you to come to me so I can see you again and ask you out? Without interference from anyone else?"

Suddenly an idea popped into his head, and he got a wicked grin on his face.

"That just might do it. It's taking a big chance that she will get insulted and just walk out the door, but I'm betting she's just as intrigued by this attraction as I am."

He toasted his phone with his coffee. "Until tomorrow, Tegan O'Neill."

Twelve

Tegan waved at Patti, then at some of the other moms she knew, including Juanita, when she dropped her kids off at their schools on Monday morning. She drove back home and settled down in her office with a cup of coffee and turned on her computer to input the receipts Patti had given her for all of the food ingredients she had bought for the party. Tegan was working on finishing up the final statement for Friday night's party when the phone rang.

"Hello," she said, while she continued to type numbers onto her screen.

"Hello, Tegan," Alexander's voice sounded like a cross between a purr from a large, dangerous cat and an invitation. "I trust you slept well over the weekend, and you are already jumping into a new workweek, as I am."

Trying not to sound as excited as she felt, Tegan tried to modulate her voice, saying, "Why yes, actually, I am getting a lot done. I'm finishing up the final statement for your party. Would you like me to fax you a copy of it?"

"No, I have a much better idea. Why don't you drop by my office later today, and you can give it to me, and I can give you your check."

Tegan felt her heart start to pound at the thought of seeing him again so soon.

"I'm not sure I can make it today. Can't you just mail it to me?" Alexander cleared his throat. "I don't think that would be a good idea. You see, there are some things I would like to discuss with you, to clarify some issues." He paused. "Why don't you drop by, say, around four-thirty? Most of my calls will be done and I can give you a few minutes then."

"Well, it *is* Patti's day to pick up the kids after school... but the traffic is going to be really a bitch that time of day."

There was a pause, then Alexander said smoothly, "You could come to my condo later and we could chat there without interruption."

"*No!*" Tegan squeaked. "I mean; that would be too late. I have to pick up the kids from Patti's by six, feed them dinner, then they do homework and I have to put them to bed."

Once again, she could swear she actually heard him smile into the phone. "Then I'll expect to see you at my office around four-thirty today. Bring that statement with you. Now I have another call coming in. Goodbye, Tegan."

Tegan stared at the now-dead phone, and yelled. "You asshole! You give me two unpleasant choices and make me pick one! This is some kind of game to you, isn't it?"

She slammed her phone back down in the cradle and stared at the computer screen for a while.

"I should add a whole bunch of extra bills to your statement, then see how you react when the amount is so much higher than you expect!"

She glared at her screen for a while longer and found herself getting up to use the bathroom. While she was up, she wandered into her room and began to sort through her clothes, looking for something suitable to wear to show Alexander and his ego that she was *not* the kind of woman to be bossed around.

Thirteen

As she had expected, the traffic going into the city was already backed up at three-thirty when she hit the highway. So she popped in a CD and gyrated in her seat, singing and tapping her non-driving foot, while she passed the time crawling inch-by-inch to her destination. Since it was later in the afternoon and some people had already gone home, she was able to find a parking space in the nearest parking garage a lot faster than she had the last time she had been down here, when she brought the original contract to be signed. She also noted the rates were five dollars cheaper in late afternoon, so at least there was one positive thing about this encounter.

Once she walked the block to the right building and rode up the elevator to the right floor, she saw the reception area was deserted; she was just starting to wonder how to get beyond the receptionist's desk to find Alexander's office, when the woman she had seen the last time here, reappeared at her desk, carrying her coat and purse.

"Oh! I'm sorry," she said quickly. "I didn't know there was anyone else expected today."

"I have a four-thirty appointment with Mr. Reyes," Tegan said. "Would you please let him know I'm here?"

"Of course," she said. She sat back down at her desk and hit some buttons on her telephone console. "Alexander? Your four-thirty appointment is here. Should I send her on through to your office or will you come to get her?"

She nodded, then hung up the phone. "He said to go right on back. Do you remember how to get to his office?"

Tegan nodded. "I think so."

The woman hit a button that unlocked the door behind her and Tegan slid her messenger bag higher on her shoulder, strode through the door and down the hall to the last office on the left.

The door was ajar, but she still knocked on it.

"Come on in."

Trying to control her nerves, Tegan took a deep breath, pushed the door open and walked into the lion's den once again.

Alexander was sitting behind his desk, ear bud and mouthpiece in place, finishing up a call, but he waved for her to come in and sit on the chair directly in front of his desk where she had sat the last time. He was dressed in a long-sleeved shirt with rolled-up sleeves, and just looking at the dark hair on his arms unnerved her. He had loosened his tie, too, and when she saw the black chest hair that peeked up from under his open collar, she remembered what it had felt like, crushed against her skin, and she hurriedly looked away from him. She sat down, smoothing out the wrinkles in her skirt, and demurely crossed her ankles over each other, her hands folded in her lap. She was aware this was a classic protection position in body language, but she didn't care. She was not in her element here; she was in his.

She looked around his office as, once again, she was kept waiting by his incessant phone calls. There were no family pictures around, just generic-looking landscapes of the desert areas out west. There were a few vases and bowls that looked like they had been bought in New Mexico and a small end table with trade magazines on it was covered with a colorful serape.

She felt a quick urge to strip naked and wrap herself in that serape, thinking to finally force this man to hang up and pay attention to her, when she became aware he wasn't talking anymore and was removing the headset.

He punched a few buttons on his phone console and smiled at her. "Now any calls will go to my answering machine. So we can talk, uninterrupted."

"Is there anyone else still in the office at this time of day?" she asked, since most of the offices she had passed had been dark and empty. She was almost afraid of the answer, since she wasn't sure she wanted to be so alone with him.

He shrugged. "There's a few of us who do business with people in vastly different time zones. That's why I have an office in my condo as well. But I'm usually one of the last ones to leave here."

He gave her a mischievous smile. "Why, does it bother you that we might be alone up here?"

Briskly, Tegan answered. "No, of course not. I brought along that statement I told you about, that I finished up this afternoon. Here it is." She slid the paper across his desk and was pleased with the barely concealed look of lust that flashed across his face as her movement allowed him a quick glance at her cleavage.

He took the paper and appeared to study it before putting it down in front of him. "It looks comprehensive. And I have something for you."

He opened a drawer, took out a check and slid it across the desk at her. She looked at the amount written on it, then let out a gasp. She looked up at him in surprise and he could see the instant she made the leap in the wrong direction, as the color rose in her face and she flushed a bright shade of red.

"I can't accept this."

He leaned back in his chair. "And why not? You and your partner did an excellent job on the party. Everything was delivered as promised, and I got the client's account. I promised you a bonus if I got it, so that's reflected in the check."

Tegan's face was still flushed as she angrily told him, "You *know* why I can't take this. How dare you insult me by paying me extra for what happened at the party? Who the hell do you think you are?"

He leaned forward. "Tegan, that's what I was afraid you were going to think. That's why I wanted you to come in person to pick up the check. Honey, the money has nothing to do with what happened between us. This is just business. You have no idea what kind of money this account will bring into my company. I got a five-thousand dollar bonus check from my boss this afternoon after the client signed the contract with me. Since your party was so instrumental in proving to him that I can take care of his every need, I thought it was only fair to share the wealth by giving your company ten percent of my bonus. That's all. You and Patti earned it. I will be insulted if you don't take it."

She looked at him intently, then decided he wasn't lying. She took the check and put it into her bag. "Okay, you win. It's made out to our company. I'm going to cash it. So nice doing business with you. Thanks so much. Now I really have to be going."

She got up and turned to leave, but Alexander rose and reached across his desk to grab her wrist. "Tegan, please wait. That's not the only reason I wanted you to come here. Hear me out."

She looked at his hand gripping her arm and looked up into his eyes. He dropped his hand, but walked around the desk to lean against it on the same side she was on. She sat back down.

"This is so awkward," he began; taking a deep breath he continued. "I'm not usually at a loss for words, but I'm not sure what to say that will convince you to see me again."

She raised her eyebrows at him. "I'm seeing you right now, aren't I?"

He smiled at her. "You are deliberately misconstruing what I mean. You *know* what I mean. I want to take you out to dinner. I want a chance to prove to you that I really *can* control myself, usually. I have never before acted like I did the other night, and I want to make it up to you."

He took her hand in his and gently massaged her knuckles before raising her hand to his lips and kissing those same knuckles.

"I want to have the opportunity to spend some time enjoying you and making you scream again. Will you give me a chance?"

She sighed heavily, then asked him. "You don't have any children, do you?"

He looked at her in surprise. "No."

"But you are divorced?"

"Yes."

"It must have been so easy for you. Only the two of you involved... clean and hardly messy at all. I was married for fifteen years, and two years ago, my happily-ever-after exploded in my face. I had to deal with my own pain, as well as my nine and six-year old children's pain. They are still not over it. I'm not sure if they will ever be over it."

He waited quietly, while she thought of what to say next.

"What I mean is, I won't allow them to get attached to another man who will then desert them when he gets tired of me. I can understand what's going on, but they can't. They shouldn't have to. They've already had to deal with too much pain in their short lives."

She looked up earnestly into his eyes and saw understanding competing with desire. "You know what I mean, don't you?"

He nodded. "Would you consider seeing me if they didn't know about it?"

She nodded. "I might."

"Do they ever spend time with their father?"

"Yes. They spend one weekend a month with their dad in his apartment in the city."

He felt his pulse begin to race. "Is there one of those weekends in the near future?"

She nodded again. "This weekend. He'll pick them up after school on Friday. Then he'll drop them off back home on Sunday around dinner time."

"What time should I pick you up for dinner on Friday?"

She shook her head. "I'm not sure that's a good idea either. We live in a very in-bred sub-division, with everyone poking their noses into everyone else's business. I know your brother and his wife... I was in a playgroup with Juanita."

His smile was partly wicked, partly guilty and not at all understandable to her. "So I heard."

She continued. "So, if this is going to happen at all, I don't want anyone else to know about it. If anyone in the neighborhood knows, they will talk about it. Their kids will hear it. Their kids will tell my kids. And that's not going to happen. Do you understand?"

He looked bemused. "Yes, you want to sneak around to see me, like we are having an affair."

"Which is what we will be doing. Having an affair, I mean. Nothing more."

He looked closely at her, studying her face. "Do you really think you can keep your emotions in check like that?"

A sly smile played around her lips. "Of course. I had other lovers before my husband. I haven't had a purely sexual relationship since before I met him in college, but I haven't forgotten how."

He appeared to be deep in thought. "Purely sexual? No strings attached?"

She nodded. "That's the best I can offer. Take it or leave it."

He moved so fast she didn't have time to react before he had pulled her up and out of her chair. He grabbed the back of her head with one hand and his other hand fondled her butt as he pressed himself into her, showing her what just being in the same room with her was doing to him. He lowered his head to brush her lips with his, then he took full possession of her lips and crushed them, forcing her mouth to open, to take his tongue into battle with her own. She responded without thinking, her hands running up and down his back, from his hard shoulder muscles to his even harder butt muscles, and she felt his hands on her again, setting her skin on fire wherever he slid them under her clothes.

She gasped and pushed him away. "No! Not yet!"

He panted as if he had been running. "Why? You don't like desks? What about the couch over there?"

She laughed. "No, desks are fine. But I got my period on Saturday. I'm only half-way done with it."

He groaned, then sat back against his desk and took both of her hands in his, looking into her eyes. "I should have used a condom with you on Friday. If there had been any blood left in my brain, I would have realized that. But there wasn't. I'm sorry again for being such an animal with you."

She smiled conspiratorially at him. "I told you, it's okay. Not only was it the only sex I've had for years, but it was damn hot sex, too! You won't hear any complaints from me!"

He shook his head. "You are an amazing woman, Tegan. Why the hell did your ex-husband ever let you go?"

She got a guarded look on her face. "That's a long story, and it's private. I may tell you sometime, but not now."

He nodded. "I respect your privacy. I will take any part of you that you offer to me. If it's only one weekend a month, I will take it. Agreed?"

She nodded back to him. "Agreed."

She looked slyly up at him. "Should we shake on it?"

He looked at her in alarm. "No! I don't trust myself to touch you anymore today."

He walked back around his desk to sit down in his chair, a wicked glint in his eyes. "But come Friday night, you belong to me, Tegan O'Neill."

She smiled at him as she got up and turned to leave.

He watched her walk to the door, then she turned when he spoke again.

"I'll call you early Friday to let you know when and where to meet me for dinner. Is there any kind of food you really dislike?"

She nodded. "I don't do seafood. I love red meat, even though it's not good for me."

He continued. "And music? Is there anything you especially like or dislike?"

She smiled. "I *hate* rap, country and disco. I *love* blues, salsa, hard rock and anything with screaming guitar solos."

He sighed. "Where have you been all of my life?"

She giggled. "Having a life of my own. And waiting for you to find me, I guess."

"Until Friday, then?"

"Bye, Alex. See you then."

He went over to his door as she walked down the hall so he could watch her butt while she made her way to the exit. She turned, smiled and waved, then walked through the door to the reception area and the elevators.

Alexander realized he was rubbing himself as he watched her walk, and he looked guiltily around, glad to see there wasn't anyone else around to notice. He walked back to his office to gather his things and leave for the day. He was thinking aloud all the while about where to take Tegan on Friday for the public part of their evening. He couldn't think about what would happen after he got her to his condo, or he would be unable to walk, what with the seam in his pants already cutting off the circulation to his engorged organ.

"Dinner and music at the 'House of Blues'? Or should I call Buddy and see who's playing at his place Friday? Or how about taking her to my favorite Mexican place, then for some salsa dancing? The only problem there is that if I do the cha-cha with her in public, I might have to take her right on the dance floor! It had better be a poorly-lit place, so no one notices! Yeah, right; who am I kidding? The way she screams, everyone will know. But who cares? I sure don't. *¡Dios mío!* I want that woman so bad!"

Once he was in his car and starting out of the garage, he was struck with a terrible thought, "She only wants a purely sexual relationship. But I'm already halfway in love with her. Now what?"

As he shifted into gear and hit the road running, he thought to himself, "I have to use every skill I have to make her fall in love with me. Am I up to it? I think so! Tegan, my dear, there's nothing I like more than a challenge!" And once again, he smiled.

Fourteen

Tegan always hated the last-minute rushing around that took place in her house one Friday a month when the kids were getting ready to spend the weekend with their dad. They both had toothbrushes and pajamas and a few changes of clothes at his apartment, but they needed to bring their pillows, their sleeping bags and their homework with them. Katie was insisting on bringing her personal CD player with her and was panicked to find her batteries were dead. So there was a frantic search for new batteries, which were found not in the junk drawer where they belonged, but in the silverware drawer, where Kevin had hidden them to keep them for his game-boy. This led to yelling between them and it was with relief Tegan answered the door when the doorbell rang.

She had taken John's key away from him when he had moved out. They had established a relationship based on mutual tolerance, but there were no friendly overtones on her part. John had asked her to consider still being his friend, since they had spent so much of their lives together, but at first the pain had been too raw for her to do that. Now that more time had passed, she wasn't still angry with him, but she hadn't forgiven him enough to treat him as more than an acquaintance who had once been important to her. For the sake of the children, she was polite to him, but she wanted it clear to all of them, especially to Katie, there was *no* possibility of them ever becoming a family again.

"Hello, Tegan," John said as she opened the door. "Sounds loud in there."

"Hi, John," she said as he walked into the house. "A minor catastrophe, once again narrowly avoided because I always keep more batteries in the house."

"You have always been so good at keeping things under control," John observed as the kids kept yelling at each other while they dragged their things down the stairs into the living room. "Sometimes I wish I was as organized as you are."

She looked at him closely. "Is that a compliment? Be still, my beating heart."

He looked uncomfortable and there was an awkward silence.

"How's Bill these days?" she asked, her tone indicating she really didn't care about the answer.

"He's fine, thanks for asking," John continued. "Are you seeing anyone yet?"

She regarded him with raised eyebrows. "Why? Feeling guilty, are you?"

He shook his head. "No, but I think two years is long enough for you to mourn what is long over and to think about finding someone new to make you happy."

"There's always 'Mr. Happy,' remember? And it's too hard to date with the kids around… finding a sitter is difficult and expensive," she told him. "Besides, I'm not going to have them get attached to anyone new so they can be hurt again when he gets tired of me, too."

"You are not the kind of woman most men would get tired of, Tegan," he told her quietly.

She looked at him in surprise. "Two compliments in one day? Are you feeling okay? Maybe it's just a fever or something."

He smiled ruefully at her and quickly added, before the kids got too close. "Think about it, though. I have someone in my life. You should, too."

"Thanks for the advice, 'Dad'," she sneered back at him. "But if I needed advice on my love-life, or lack of one, you'd be the last one I'd think of asking."

Then the kids were next to them, hugging their dad, hugging their mom and demanding their full attention. It took all four of them to carry all of the stuff the kids needed for the weekend out to the car. Once they were all settled in, Tegan backed away from the car and waved at them.

"See you on Sunday," she told them. "Katie, you be sure and do all of your homework. Ask your dad to help you with your math; after all, that was his major in college. And don't turn those headphones on so loud that other people can hear the music or you'll burst your eardrums. Kevin, no playing computer games all night again like you did the last time. Remember, you were late to school on Monday because you couldn't get out of bed."

The car pulled out of the driveway as the kids leaned out of the windows yelling, "Bye Mom! See you Sunday!"

"Have fun," she yelled at them, as they headed off down the street.

She turned, walked back into the house and closed the door. And then, remembering she had something to look forward to that night, instead of feeling the beginnings of her usual depression when the house was quiet, she smiled to herself, saying aloud. "Now that the cats are away, it's time for the mouse to play!" And she headed into her room to pack for the weekend.

Fifteen

Tegan drove to a commuter lot by the airport and parked, which allowed her to leave her car there for twenty-four hours. After all, she figured, if things didn't work out well with Alex, that would give her a reason to leave by late Saturday afternoon. And if things were going well, she would just ask him to drive her out to the lot so she could put more money into the collection machine so her car wouldn't get towed. She caught the el and rode downtown with her messenger bag on the seat next to her. She had brought one change of clothes, a couple of pairs of underwear, a toothbrush and some makeup. On a whim, she tossed in a few pieces of lingerie, but she wasn't sure if she would have the guts to be that inventive with Alex yet.

"Who am I kidding?" she had thought to herself as she looked it over, "He's seen me in lingerie already, and he liked what he saw then! And I liked what seeing me in it did to him, so maybe I *will* find a way to wear some."

Then she had taken a quick shower and put on another lacy black bra and thong set, along with her garter belt and stockings. She sprayed a little perfume under her breasts and between her legs, along with the sides of her neck. She applied minimal makeup and brushed her short hair, then surveyed herself in the mirror.

"Not bad for an almost-forty year old," she told herself. She slipped on her favorite black dress that managed to accentuate her curves, show off her cleavage and yet cover up the fact her abdomen still showed the effects of two pregnancies and c-sections. Since it was still early in fall, it wasn't really cold outside during the day, but it did get chilly at night, so she slipped on her trench coat, smiling at the memory it would surely bring back to Alex.

"It's my only good fall coat," she told herself defensively. "And I can't be seen walking around downtown in this dress without getting arrested for solicitation!"

So after riding the el down to the exit she had chosen as closest to Buddy Guy's Legends, where Alex wanted her to meet him at eight for dinner, she found a cab and was whisked to the front door of the club. She walked into the club and was instantly assailed by the sounds of blues music being piped into the air, since the live music didn't start until much later. She told the hostess she was here to meet someone and was surprised when the hostess said, "Of course, Ms. O'Neill, right this way."

She followed the hostess to a table that had an excellent view of the stage, yet was a booth, with privacy for people who might want to touch each other while they watched the rest of the room. She was embarrassed he might see what she was thinking on her face, so she tried to look nonchalant. Alex saw her and jumped up to welcome her to his table by taking her bag away from her, putting it on the booth behind him, and then taking her hand in his and kissing the knuckles. He turned her hand around then and quickly licked her palm before he gestured for her to slide into the booth before him.

Tegan was trying to get over the shock that feeling his tongue on her skin had given her, while she watched Alex pour some champagne into the two glasses on the table.

"Champagne?" She asked, willing her voice to stop shaking. "What's the occasion?"

He smiled at her as he handed her a glass, then clinked his glass to hers. "A toast, to your saying yes to meeting me, and to the first of what I hope will be many yeses."

They both took a sip of their champagne and she was surprised at how much she liked the taste of what she knew by the label to be an expensive brand.

"Did you have any trouble getting down here and finding a parking space?" he asked.

"I can't afford to park down here," she answered. "I left my car in a commuter lot by the airport and paid for twenty-four hours of parking. Then I'll have to either redeem my car or pay for another day."

He raised his eyebrows as he smiled at her. "Is that a ploy, so that if you are *not* enjoying being with me, you'll have an excuse to leave… so you can go rescue your car before it gets towed?"

She flushed before she answered him. "You really *are* an arrogant bastard, aren't you?"

"Well, my parents were married right before I was born, so the second part of that isn't true. But I'm a Hispanic man, Tegan, I'm the oldest son in my family and an alpha-male. They don't come much more aggressive than me. I've found I can usually get my own way and what I want, by just pursuing it hard enough. So yes, I guess I *am* arrogant. Does that bother you?"

She studied him then, her eyes seeming to examine him as closely as a bug under the microscope. "No, I don't think so. I'm too old and confident myself, to be afraid of you. And I also know I have something you want. So since I've already figured out this is a game to you, that you like to chase, and I'm the prey, I'll just have to try to stay a couple of steps in front of you so you won't get bored too quickly."

He laughed a hearty, pleased sound that reflected his enjoyment of her company. "God, it's good to be with a real woman. I'm getting sick and tired of little girls who are either too afraid of me to stand up to me, or just interested in getting right to bed, without having any fun getting there. You make me laugh, and believe it or not, I've been spending so much time thinking about how much I want to be with you again, it's been affecting my work ethic all week."

"Then I guess it's good I already cashed that huge check you gave me, huh? That way if your job is in jeopardy, at least I'll get mine first."

He poured more champagne into both of their glasses, then leaned over to gently brush her lips with his. She was shocked at how much the smallest touch of his lips affected her, making her feel like her bones were melting and liquid was pooling in her thong.

He leaned over further, to trail his lips and then his tongue along her face to her ear, then down her neck. He whispered into her ear. "You'll get yours first, all right. And I plan to make sure you scream yourself hoarse this weekend, so don't expect to be able to do much talking when your kids get home on Sunday. You'll just have to tell them you have a sore throat, and use sign language to communicate with them."

"Ooh, a sore throat, huh? And I'll bet you have just the thing for me to suck on to make myself feel better!"

She ran her hand along the length of him, their laps covered by the white tablecloth. There was a sharp intake of breath as he tried to recover enough to be able to talk again. Instead, he reached one hand behind her head into her hair and tilted her head back so he could kiss her long and hard, making her taste the longing that had been torturing him all week. Some long, sweaty moments later, he released her and leaned back to wipe his forehead with his napkin.

"Good lord, woman, you make me sweat! And that dress of yours? When I saw you walk in wearing that, suddenly the concept of a little black dress made sense to me for the first time ever. I almost levitated the table, I got so hard thinking about what must be under it. You're wearing garters again, aren't you?"

He ran his hand up and down her thighs under her dress. She gasped when he moved the thong aside to push the tip of one finger into her.

He smiled at her. "Do you want me to make you come before we order dinner? I can do it, you know. I'll just move my finger around a little bit, like this."

He swirled his finger around, and despite her best intentions to control herself, she felt herself start to quiver, then she moaned softly as she closed her eyes and gave herself over to a mini-orgasm that made bursts of light appear on the insides of her eyelids. She felt his lips on hers again, and responded like they were old lovers, like they both knew just what the other one wanted.

Reluctantly, Tegan pushed herself away from him. "We'd better be careful! I hear that public indecency charges are a bitch to fight in the city. But if you don't stop doing that, I'm going to climb on top of you and have my way with you right here in the booth. And I don't think there is a tablecloth big enough to cover up what we'd be doing."

Alexander laughed softly and poured more champagne into their glasses. "Another toast, my dear. To the rest of the night and to the pleasures to come. And come, and come!"

Tegan giggled, then took another sip from her glass as the waitress appeared to take their order. They ordered, and soon after, the food began arriving, so they concentrated on taking care of the one appetite they could safely satisfy in public. As they ate, they chatted about various things, including their jobs, the state of world politics and books they had recently read.

"It's so good to talk to someone else who reads actual books," Alex said, as they argued over whether or not there should be any sequels to the Harry Potter series and of the difficulty of translating an author's vision to a movie.

Tegan nodded. "All my kids want to do is use Spark Notes.com... today's version of the Cliff notes we used to have... remember those yellow books that meant you didn't have to read the entire book in order to pass the test?"

"Yeah, but I didn't really use them much until I got to college. I was working full-time while I was going to school full-time and I had very little time to do my homework, if I ever wanted to sleep. I couldn't figure out why, when I wanted to get a business degree, I had to take all of the Gen. Ed. crap, like English one-oh-one and Philosophy. Turns out those were some of my favorite classes, even though they had absolutely *no* bearing on what I was there to study. And it was always easy to get laid in an English class. I'd just talk with a heavy Spanish accent, telling the girls I was having trouble with understanding the words in the books we had to read and asking them to help me after class."

Tegan laughed. "You must have been a real lady-killer back then. You're still a very attractive man. And you have no accent whatsoever, so that must have been some act on your part!"

They both finished their coffee as the flashing of the lights indicated the band was going to be starting soon. Alex waved at their waitress and ordered another bottle of champagne, while Tegan made a quick trip to the bathroom in order to be back for the band. She was astounded when she returned to find that Buddy Guy himself was sitting in her seat.

When Alex saw her, he smiled and Buddy rose to greet her. "So, this is the woman you wanted to impress by bringing her to my club, huh, Alex?"

"Yes, Buddy, this is Tegan O'Neill. Tegan, this is my old friend Buddy Guy."

Weakly she smiled, then slid into the seat next to Alex as Buddy stood in front of them. "I just stopped by to be sure the staff was treating my man Alex right. And to have a look at the woman he wanted to show off. Man, oh man, Alex, you don't deserve this one! She has way too much class for you, home-boy. Tegan, honey, if you ever want a *real* man, make sure you give me a call!"

The waitress returned with their new bottle of champagne and Buddy looked over to the stage and nodded at the stage manager. "I've got to get up there and introduce the band. Tegan, if you can get away from this wetback long enough, I'd really like to have a dance with you tonight."

She smiled at Buddy. He walked back to the stage and she watched as Alex poured them some cold champagne. "You planned that, didn't you? Told him to flatter me and all? This is all a part of your seduction plan, right?"

Alex shook his head slowly and frowned. "No, I only asked him to save me this table and to be sure I got the most efficient waitress. Buddy *never* dances with anyone in his club. That was his idea, and I'm not so sure I like it at all. I don't want any other man touching you, tonight or any other night."

She shook her head and patted his face. "Tsk, tsk. That macho-man possessiveness is going to get you into trouble some day. And truly, it's been so long since *any* man wanted to touch me I don't think you have much to worry about. Besides," she continued touching him, but now much lower than his face. "I want my sunglasses back and I

64

intend to search your place until I find them. Don't think I don't know you have them. You returned the boom box, but not the glasses."

He smiled wickedly at her. "I'm holding them for ransom. This way you have to come over to my place and once I have you in there, I don't intend to let you leave until I've had my way with you, as many times, and in as many positions, as I can think of. And baby, I have a *very* vivid imagination!"

He leaned over and kissed her, and they groped each other under cover of darkness, as the stage lights came on and the floor lights were turned down. The band started to play and once they listened for a few songs, Alex inclined his head towards the dance floor. That was all the invitation Tegan needed.

Alex already knew Tegan was a good dancer, but she was pleasantly surprised to find so was he, and he could follow her lead or take over, as the mood struck both of them. The first three songs were quick ones and they danced all three of them, only to retreat back to their booth when a slow one started in order to catch their breath and drink more champagne. Talking wasn't easy anymore, since the band was so loud, so they drank and fondled each other until they felt ready to dance again. They danced some more, then rested. This went on until they were down to the last two glasses of champagne and the band began a very slow blues song.

Since they had not done any slow dancing, Tegan was surprised when Alex stood up and took her hand to lead her to the dance floor. He put his arms around her and held her so close she felt the hard muscles bunched up all over his body; his erection rubbed against her and she found it hard to breathe she wanted him so badly.

He said her name softly. She looked up at him and found his eyes had darkened once again, to an inky blackness that threatened to swallow her. He lowered his head to kiss her, and a low groan escaped from him.

"I can't do this anymore. I can't keep my hands off you anymore. We have to get back to my place *now*! Tell me you want that, too."

She panted as if she had just run a mile. "If you don't get me out of here soon, I'm going to take my chances with the indecency squad. That table over there is just about the same height as the desk you took me on the last time. Maybe once we work our way through the rest of the furniture, you'll finally get me into a bed."

He took her hand, led her off the dance floor and back to their booth, so she could grab her messenger bag and her purse. On their way out of the club, she saw Buddy watching them go and she waved at him; Alex nodded.

When they were outside, she was glad she had her trench coat with her since she was covered in sweat from dancing and the night air was chilly.

The valet brought Alex his car and he opened the door to let her in; there was a sharp intake of breath when her skirt slid up, revealing her garters as she slid into the car. Alex shut the door and got in on his side. Then they were off, cruising along as if they were flying.

"What a car!" Tegan said, "I don't think I've ever even been close to a Ferrari before. Do you think you might let me drive it out to the parking lot tomorrow, when I have to feed the meter for my car?"

He turned to her, a slight smile on his lips. "We'll see… I may not be willing to let you get clothes on for long enough to drive anywhere tomorrow. I'll gladly pay to get your car back, if I can keep you in my bed and naked."

He turned the music on louder and the sounds of Buddy Guy's wailing guitar took them all the way to his building, where he drove up to the parking lot on the sixth floor and parked in his spot close to the elevators.

He got out and came around the car to find she had already opened the door and grabbed her bag out of the back. He led the way to the elevators and pressed the button for up. Once the door opened, they got in and he took her bag and dropped it on the floor. His arms were around her and he was pressing her against the wall of the elevator as he kissed and groped her. He only stopped when the elevator did; he picked up her bag and led her down the hall to his condo. Then he opened the door and gestured for her to precede him into his domain.

She gasped as she entered what looked like a place right out of an interior decorating magazine. Tasteful leather furniture was everywhere and a corner fireplace was surrounded by glass, so that if you were seated on the fur-covered futon in front of it, you were looking at the fire as well as out the windows onto the skyline of Chicago. The dining room table was made of glass and metal and everything in the place screamed of money and no children around to break anything. The plush carpet was so inviting Tegan gratefully kicked off her heels, letting her tired feet be soothed by the softness of the floor covering. There were paintings around the room, most of which appeared to be original artwork. There was a huge painting of a voluptuous dark-skinned nude woman reclining on a beach, right over one of the couches. She was still lost in looking around when Alex appeared at her side with an ice bucket holding a bottle of champagne, the same kind they had been drinking, and two glasses.

He smiled at her, then gestured with the hand holding the glasses for her to follow him over to the futon in front of the fireplace. Once there, he sat down and she sat beside him. He picked up what looked like a remote control device and hit some buttons. The lights dimmed, the sound of Buddy Guy's guitar filled the air, although Alex turned the sound down so they could still hear each other, and the fireplace was instantly lit with the wood starting to crackle from the real fire.

"How did you do that?" she asked him, nodding at the fireplace.

He smiled. "Electric ignition for the gas, then they both shut off and the fire takes over." He popped the champagne open and poured some into both glasses, handing her one.

"Another toast? To how beautiful you look by the light of the fire."

They both took a drink, then he said, "Tegan, you really are a beautiful woman. Buddy was right... you do have too much class for me. I have no right to expect anything from you, but I'm going to anyway, because that's the kind of arrogant bastard I am."

They both smiled as he took her glass out of her hand and put both glasses down on the table next to him. He turned to her and leaned over to kiss her, softly, gently, then more insistently until just as the fire had done, their passion ignited and they both began to frantically remove each other's clothing.

She got his jacket off, then his tie. She began to unbutton his shirt and leaned close to inhale the smell of him, as she licked at his skin, then circled wet kisses around each of his nipples in turn. He moaned as she finished with his shirt and pulled it off him. He reached behind her and unzipped her dress, sliding it down her shoulders to reveal the black lace bra he was hoping to find.

"Black suits you so well," he panted, rubbing her nipples through the thin, silky fabric. "Your skin is so white that the contrast makes me crazy!"

He pulled her on his lap and she put one thigh on either side of his as she rubbed herself on his erection and leaned over to kiss him. Their tongues dueled, darting in and out of each other's mouth. She moaned as he undid her bra with one hand so he could slide it off her, setting her breasts free. He leaned forward and took first one, then the other nipple into his mouth and licked and sucked her until she lost the ability to think of anything other than the feeling of his mouth and hands on her. Suddenly she shuddered and moaned, as an orgasm caught her by surprise.

He laughed softly. "Shall we try to keep count, Tegan? Or do you just want me to keep you coming all night?"

She looked at him, her blue eyes cloudy with a dreamy, unfocussed look in them, saying, "All night? How about all weekend?"

"Your wish is my command, Mistress," he said, then pushed her on to her back and eased her dress over her hips and off her entirely. This left her wearing only a black lace thong and garter belt with silk stockings. She slowly stretched out, her arms overhead, arching her back and sighing softly.

He stood up and removed his pants, carefully unzipping them over his bulging erection. "You look like a wet dream, woman. Like what I used to conjure up in my imagination to masturbate to when I was a teenager. I have no idea how I got lucky enough to get you up here, but I intend to enjoy you in more ways than you can even imagine. Starting now."

With that, he knelt in front of her and pulled off her thong, leaving only the garter belt and stockings. He leaned forward and inhaled deeply while he spread her thighs open to see she was glistening with moisture, ready for him and eager.

"You smell so good! Let's see how you taste." He leaned forward even more and his tongue licked at her... first flicking gently, then lapping with more force as she moaned and thrashed, making him have to hold her thighs still so he could continue his assault on her senses. As his tongue drove her mad, causing orgasms she couldn't control to overwhelm her, he poked first one, then two fingers into her, enjoying the feel of the muscles that gripped him and made him want, no *need* to be inside of her *now*!

With a low groan, he backed away and fumbled in his pants pocket for a condom.

She was lying back trying to remember how to breathe as he rolled it onto himself.

He slowly eased into her, backing up, then pushing forward, to make room for himself.

She screamed as an orgasm made her muscles clench and tighten around the battering ram that filled her so completely.

He wrapped his hands around her hips and pulled her against him, so that only her head and shoulders were still on the futon. Using strength she had only guessed he had, the cords of muscle stood out in his neck, arms and his thighs as he withdrew, then pushed forward again, each time filling her up more and more, pushing himself further into her until he felt the mouth of her womb, tilting towards him in welcome.

That was his undoing, as the wet, silken vise squeezing him was joined by the nub of her cervix that seemed to slurp greedily at him, urging him to fill her completely with his seed. With a shout torn out of his soul, he drove himself into her one final time, then shuddered with the strength of the orgasm that exploded out of him.

For the first time in his life, he felt what a multiple orgasm must be like, as her muscles kept on squeezing him, milking him for every drop, causing her to scream repeatedly.

She pulled him along with her, riding the waves of her pleasure, over and over again.

Time stopped for both of them and it was an eternity before he collapsed on top of her, gasping for breath, knowing he was crushing her with his weight, but unable to do anything about it. His muscles were unable to respond to any command he might have given them that didn't involve quivering.

After some time, he was able to think again and he reached down to hold onto the rubber as he slipped his still-partially-erect organ out of her, tied off the condom and dropped it to the side. She was lying back looking unconscious; her eyes fluttered and her breath still came in gasps. He sat beside her, picked up a glass and gratefully took a sip of the cool bubbly.

He leaned over and asked her. "Are you alright, my love? You didn't pass out, did you?"

She opened her eyes and smiled up at him. "I might have, I don't remember. Oh my God, you are magnificent! I'm glad you don't expect me to be able to count my orgasms, since I have no idea how many that was!"

He reached over, helped her to sit up and handed her the other glass of champagne. "Here, restore yourself. The night is still young."

She moved around on the futon. "I'm leaking all over your furniture."

He smiled at her. "No problem. The cover is washable and even if it wasn't, I don't care. I intend to have you on every piece of furniture I own, then I'll go buy some more, so I can have you on that, too. You are an amazing woman and I fully intend to do my best to tire you out. By the time you leave here on Sunday, you won't be able to walk anymore, let alone have a voice left to talk with. It will probably take us both four weeks to recover, so you can come over here again next month and we can do this all over again."

She smiled hopefully at him. "Promise?"

He used his finger to trace an X over his heart. "Cross my heart and hope to die if I lie." He poured some more champagne into their glasses and leaned back, saying companionably, "I'm thinking we hit the Jacuzzi next, then I'll show you my king-sized water bed. But don't get any ideas about sleeping on it. At least not until you make *me* pass out from pleasure. And I warn you, my girl…" he waggled a finger in front of her face, "…it's been a really long time since I've had any woman at all. It's been backed up into my brain for quite a while, so it might take you until sometime tomorrow to get me to slow down."

She smiled at him. "I thought you men were supposed to slow down once you got past forty."

He gave her a wounded look. "What makes you think I'm past forty?"

She laughed. "What, you're really only twenty-two, but this is what lots of energetic sex has done to you?"

They both laughed.

"Okay, I'm forty-two. But my libido keeps on telling me I'm still a teenager. I've always had an extremely high sex drive. I've never met a woman who could keep up with me, though you are showing great promise."

She patted the side of his face. "That's probably because you mistakenly thought only young flibberty-gibbets could have the energy to satisfy you. You forgot that an older, more experienced woman not only knows many, many ways to satisfy you the younger ones haven't learned yet, but I know how to satisfy myself as well, which in turn leads to more pleasure for you. Stick to women closer to your own age, Mister Reyes. That's my advice."

He leaned over to kiss her, then trailed his tongue along the side of her face to her ear, whispering into it, "Are you old enough for me? How about I stick to only you from now on, Ms. O'Neill? "

Panting again, she stroked his arms, then his back and then his neck as he leaned over to begin seducing her again. "I won't be forty for a few months. But I suppose I can fit you into my schedule for a while."

He lifted his head to smile at her, as she added, "Didn't you say something about a Jacuzzi?"

Sixteen

Alexander opened his eyes in the morning and was surprised at being filled with a deep feeling of well-being. He felt none of the usual stress that struck him in the head when he awoke. Instead, he felt calm and centered emotionally, and very, very horny! Since that last part wasn't unusual, he touched himself casually, then realized Tegan was still asleep next to him. He rolled over and looked at her, studying her face, listening to her gentle breathing. He moved the sheet off her, so he could admire the curve of her backside since she was lying on her stomach. He had always loved to look at women with generous curves... *must be a cultural thing*, he had often thought. And this woman had such beautiful lines to her, that if he had been a painter, he'd have begged her to model for him.

Instead, he carefully got out of bed, so as not to wake her, and went into the bathroom. He padded naked into his kitchen and made some coffee. Half-heartedly, he listened to the messages causing the lights on his phone console to blink. But once the coffee machine signaled it was done, he hit "save," since there would be plenty of time for him to get back to business once Tegan went home on Sunday afternoon. Now the only business he wanted to get back to was the business of pleasuring them both.

Realizing he was hungry, and she would be too, he picked up his cell phone and dialed the room service extension for the building. He ordered a full breakfast of eggs, bacon, potatoes, toast and fruit and asked that it be added to his tab. When they told him it would be about a forty-five minute wait, he smiled into the phone.

"That's fine. Just leave it outside the door if no one answers when you knock."

Once he had hung up, he said to himself, "That gives me just enough time to wake her up properly." He poured two cups of coffee, adding milk to hers, since he had noticed last night she liked hers that way. And he headed back into his bedroom.

Tegan was still asleep, and still on her stomach. He sat down beside her, which caused some rolling of the waterbed, and she stirred slightly. He held the cup of coffee close to her nose and said, "Wake up, sleepyhead. It's time for round two in this game of ours."

She opened her eyes and smiled at him, pushing herself up just enough to take the cup and a small sip of the coffee. "You remembered the milk. How thoughtful you are. A consummate host. I think I'll have to come back to this hotel the next time I'm in town."

He ran one hand up and down on her backside. "You are such a beautiful woman, Tegan. Roll over and let me admire the front of you as well."

She knitted her eyebrows. "But the back view is better than the front view."

"Why?"

She sighed. "Because I had two large babies, and needed to have two c-sections. There's skin hanging over the scars, and that bulge will never go away unless I inherit enough money to be able to afford the vanity of plastic surgery. And that's not even mentioning the stretch marks!"

He gently pushed her over. "I saw everything about you last night. Granted, the light was dimmer," he smiled at her raised eyebrows, "but I still think you are beautiful — even in broad daylight."

She sighed as she lay there, exposed to his eyes, resigned to his disapproval. She took another sip of coffee, raising her head and shoulders up as she did so.

"See," he said, rubbing her abdomen, "Your stomach muscles are bulging under your skin. You are in much better shape than women half your size. And I'm Hispanic, Tegan. We like our women rounder than most American men. You should see my *madre*! But then, she had eight more kids after me. So she has even more of an excuse for rounded hips than you do. And don't think she ever lets my dad forget that!"

With that, he leaned over and kissed her abdomen, licking a wet trail to her belly button. He looked up at her as he traced a path with his tongue up to each breast in turn, then to her lips. She sighed as she gave herself over to his kisses, and they made smooth, satisfying love in the late morning sunlight that came through his windows.

Afterwards, when they were lying in each other's arms, relearning how to breathe again, he said, "I think our breakfast is here. I swear I heard the doorbell ring a while ago, but you were screaming so loud that I'll have to go check to be sure."

She looked at him in surprise. "Wow! You get room service in your condo?"

When he nodded as he got out of bed, she said, "Jeez! How the other half lives! Must be nice to have all that money and only yourself to take care of with it."

He grabbed a pair of gym shorts from a dresser drawer and said, "I work hard for my money. What I need is someone to help me enjoy spending it. So far, you are doing well on the application process, though I'm going to need to spend some more time carefully examining your qualifications. Choosing to stay naked while we eat will be a very big plus for you. Think about it while I go fetch breakfast."

She stuck out her tongue and threw a pillow at him as he walked out of the room. She could hear him laughing as he walked down the hall.

Later, after they had eaten their fill while sitting at his dining room table, he said, "Let's go sit by the fireplace again and I'll open the balcony door and we can check out the skyline in daylight."

"You don't want me to sit out there naked, do you?" She asked with trepidation, as they carried their coffee over to admire the view. "I don't mind *you* looking at me, but I really have to draw the line at the rest of the neighborhood. You never know when the paparazzi will be around. And there's no way I want my kids finding out about us by seeing my picture on the front page of the paper, under the headline, 'Local business woman provides *full-service* to satisfied customer'."

He moved himself closer to her on the futon and put his arm around her, using his other hand to tilt her head up so that he could kiss her.

"I *am* satisfied with you, Tegan. I woke up so damn happy that I didn't feel like myself at all! I'm usually a very discontented kind of man. And driven, too."

She looked at him closely, one hand tracing the line of his face, enjoying the feel of the beard he had not shaved that morning, remembering what it had felt like on her thighs last night. She smiled at him, as he read her thoughts, and groaned, taking her hand and kissing her palm.

"Why are you so driven? You have everything you could possibly want. The condo, the car, the money. What else is there for you to work so hard for?"

"I don't know," he said shaking his head. "I told you I'm the oldest of nine kids. Both sets of grandparents lived with us while I was growing up. Most of the time there wasn't enough food for anyone to eat, so we had to share what little there was. I've eaten more beans and tortillas than I ever want to again, but I still like them. They remind me of home."

He took another sip of his coffee and looked off at the view of the city. "I swore to myself a long time ago that when I got older I wasn't ever going to live like that again, once I had a choice. I worked two jobs all the way through high school and one full-time job during college. I had to take out loans, since I wasn't really a good enough student to get much scholarship money, other than what I qualified for based on my family's income level. I've long since paid them all back, and I've put a lot of miles between me and the way I grew up. But I can't seem to get myself out of hyper-drive, so I continue to work longer hours than anyone else."

He turned back to face her. "Other than the time I've spent with you, I can't remember the last time I didn't think about work all day." He kissed her again.

"See, that's why this arrangement is so good for both of us," she said. "You need to relax. I need some good sex in my life. We can take care of each other's needs, and both be happy. This way, you still have most of the month to be your overachieving self, and I have most of the month to be a mom. Then we can play this game of ours for forty-eight hours and go back to our routines."

His lips trailed down her neck to her shoulders, as he gently pushed her over and demanded her full attention again.

Much later, he said, "Good sex? Merely *good* sex?"

Her eyes fluttered open and she forced herself to focus on his face. "Did I say *good sex*? I meant fantabulous, mind-blowing, knock-your-socks off, dear lord I stopped breathing again, and rock-my-world sex!"

He gave her a highly self-satisfied smirk. "Okay, then. Remember, us Hispanic men have huge egos. You have to stroke us a lot, or we feel neglected."

She reached over and wrapped her hand around him, as she lowered her head, saying, "Then I'd better get to that stroking thing, huh?"

He leaned back on the futon, wrapped his hands in her hair, and moaned for an answer.

Seventeen

They left the condo only to drive to the commuter lot to put more money in the machine, so Tegan's car would be safe for another twenty-four hours. Alexander had allowed Tegan to drive his car to the lot, since she knew how to get there, but he had insisted on driving it back. She had teased him about being too macho to allow a woman to be in charge of his life by driving him around. He didn't argue with her, but conceded the truth of her theory. This had led to some good-natured teasing about macho men and uppity women, and they had settled that argument with a truce, after a great deal of splashing around in the Jacuzzi.

They didn't get hungry again until it was getting dark outside. Alexander suggested they order a pizza, so they didn't need to get dressed again. Since she was enjoying being naked and not feeling ashamed of her body, Tegan agreed, though she did feel the need to tease him about it.

"Pizza, huh? I don't want you thinking you can get off cheap around me, buster. I may be easy, but I'm not cheap!"

He laughed. "After what I spent last night, my wallet needs the relief of a cheap date tonight. Plus, this way I can set your expectations lower, so it will be easier to impress you next month."

Alexander opened a bottle of Italian wine and they ate pizza and salad in his dining room while they were still naked. They made love again and again... in the Jacuzzi, on the couch in his room and once even on his balcony. He invited her out there to enjoy the view, pointing out to her that no one could see them, since the lights were out in his condo. He encouraged her to lean over the balcony to look at the lake and he entered her from behind, stroking her and whispering terms of endearment into her ear, until she screamed so loudly the neighbors turned on their lights and they quickly snuck back into his bedroom to finish their passionate encounter on his waterbed.

Soon after, they both fell asleep, totally sated, in each others' arms.

The next morning, Alexander woke up before her again. He glanced at the clock, and was astonished to see they had almost slept the entire morning away. Once again, he felt at peace with the world and lay there for a while enjoying the unusual feeling.

He woke up the woman next to him, and *allowed* her to get dressed, so they could go out to breakfast. He suggested they go to the Lincoln Park Zoo, which was a favorite place of his to walk around and think.

"I haven't been here in years," Tegan told him as they strolled around the park, looking at all of the animals out enjoying the fall sunshine. "Since we're Brookfield Zoo members, we go there instead of driving into the city. My kids love the popcorn and the zebra ice cream cones."

He smiled at her as he took her hand. "So do I. It seems I have a lot in common with them, including enjoying spending time with their mother."

She gave him an amused look. "They don't like spending time with me much lately. At least not my daughter, Katie. She's in sixth grade and beginning to find everything about me to be a source of endless embarrassment."

"But your son is younger, right? So he must still like to be with you?"

She shook her head. "Unless it involves computer games, video games or his game-boy, he doesn't like much of anything."

She sighed. "I love my kids, but sometimes I feel like they don't love me as much these days. They used to like spending time with me. Not anymore."

He stopped walking next to her, then stepped in front of her and kissed her lightly. "See, that's why you need to have a distraction in your life, so you don't expect to be totally fulfilled by them anymore."

She smiled at him. "And you *are* a major distraction, mister. You aren't the only one who had trouble concentrating on their job last week. I only hope now that I can barely walk, and barely talk, I will be able to think about other things again without the vision of you slamming your massive self into me again and again, making me unable to get anything done!"

He used his hands to hold her hips against him again, rubbing himself against her, showing her what her words had done to him.

"Damn, woman! I can't take you anywhere in public without wanting to strip you and take you on the spot!"

She giggled.

"Do you think we have enough time for a quickie in my condo before we have to get you out to your car?" He whispered hopefully into her ear, making her pulse race and her breathing speed up.

"Yes, but only if we leave now."

"Then we're out of here. We can see the rest of the animals next time."

Later, after they were dressed and she was making sure she had packed all of her things to take back home, he regarded her gravely. "Massive self? I know I'm tall, but am I too big for you?"

She laughed at him. "Now who's the one letting their insecurities show? If you were too big for me, I'd have been whimpering with pain the last couple of hundred times we made love, instead of screaming and moaning. And it's not like you don't get me ready either. So all in all, Mister Reyes, I'm completely satisfied with the first weekend of our affair. I hope you are, too. I'm already looking forward to the next one, a month from now."

He moved in front of her, tilting her head up to look at him. "The only thing I don't like is having to wait a whole month to see you again."

She shook her head. "That was the agreement. This is between you and me only. It doesn't involve my kids, so no one else finds out about it, okay? That's what we agreed on. Don't back out on me now."

"I won't. Let's go. We should have just enough time to get you back to your car before the overly-zealous parking attendants notice your time is up."

With a last look around his condo, she said, "Bye-bye, lap of luxury. I hope to see you again next month."

They took the elevator down to his car and drove to the lot where her car was. The end of their weekend was anti-climactic, and they both felt a sense of loss when they drove away from each other.

Eighteen

The first weekend after their rendezvous, Alexander tried to keep himself too busy to miss Tegan. He spent Saturday morning on the phone, scouting out more business and making calls he knew he could have left until Monday. He went to his health club, where he attacked the machines with a vengeance, until he tired himself out. After he showered, he got a massage, thinking he had always enjoyed having the hands of the massage girls on him... but even though he automatically got hard from the touch of the young woman assigned to him, he found her to be too thin, too giggly and more annoying than anything else. With a sigh, he returned to his empty condo to find he missed his new lover more than he would have thought possible after only one weekend together.

Late that evening, after he had drunk the better part of a bottle of wine with his pizza, he called her office number, thinking to avoid her children. All he got was the answering machine, so he didn't leave a message. Then he called her house number, and was dismayed when one of the kids answered the phone. After he hung up, he swore at his situation, then finished off the bottle of wine.

He opened another one and dismally looked at the calendar while he was in the kitchen, saying aloud, "I only get her one weekend out of the month! If I keep on drinking like this for the other three, I'm going to become an alcoholic. I won't be able to get it up anymore, and she'll stop wanting to be with me at all."

With that thought uppermost in his mind, he put the cork back into the second bottle and chugged a couple of glasses of water to help dilute the alcohol. He reluctantly climbed alone into his bed, where he tossed and turned for hours before he finally fell into a restless sleep.

Sunday he slept late, then woke with a headache. Thinking a shot of family might be good for him, he drove out to Aurora and invited himself to dinner at his parents' house. They were so surprised and happy to see him he felt guilty for having not called or visited in so long. He enjoyed the familiarity of his mother's nagging, his father's silence and the teasing he got from his sisters.

One of his sisters had never moved out, since she was unmarried. Anna lived with their parents, taking care of them as they had taken care of their parents. One of his other sisters, Julia, had moved back in when she got divorced. She had brought her three children with her, and that was part of the reason Alexander had taken to avoiding the house. Now he found himself watching the youngsters closely and realized the oldest niece must be close in age to Tegan's daughter, since she was easily mortified by any chance remark her mother made about her and tried to distance herself from everyone in the household.

When Lisa went out to the back porch to sit on the swing, he followed her, and under the guise of being an interested uncle, set out to find out what interested girls her age. Despite his misgivings about how to carry on a conversation with a young girl, since he had had such little luck with women just a little bit older than her twelve years, he found that as long as he was asking her questions, and really listening to the answers, it wasn't difficult to find out what she thought, and what she cared about. And he enjoyed himself a lot more than he had thought he would.

"This isn't so hard," he thought to himself, when there was a lull in their conversation. It was a companionable silence, since she was thinking about what he had told her about real men being interested in women with intelligence, even though they only seemed to care about big boobs and skinny hips. He had agreed with her how ridiculous it was for boys to expect the two physical attributes to be combined, and how rarely nature did just that. She had blossomed under his questioning; getting animated when she spoke of her favorite classes and what she hoped to major in when she got to college. Since her mother had not gone to college, he was the only person there who understood what she wanted to do with her life, and it was with reluctance on both of their parts that they went back inside for dinner.

Later, when he was relaxing with a glass of wine before bedtime, Alexander wondered, for the first time in his life, if he was missing something by not being a father. That in itself was such a bizarre notion to him, that he spent some time looking into his fireplace, pondering the idea. Sleep came a little bit easier to him that night, and as he drifted off, he imagined Tegan's warm, soft body next to him, and realized her smell was still on the pillow next to him. He snuggled into it, and fell asleep.

Nineteen

Tegan, for her part, had been totally unprepared for her daughter to be so nosy about why she seemed to be acting so strangely when her kids got back home. She didn't realize she was acting much differently than usual, until Katie asked her, while they were getting dinner ready Sunday night, what she had done with herself all weekend to put her into such a good mood.

"Why, am I usually so crabby that it's unusual for me to be happy?" she had asked defensively.

"No, but usually you miss us so much on our weekend away, that I feel guilty coming home and telling you about the good time I had with Dad. Now, I'm telling you about his taking us walking around his neighborhood, for ice cream, and we rented movies and had pizza on Saturday night; then on Sunday he took us to the zoo! You don't even seem jealous about the zoo!"

Tegan flushed, remembering that *she* had been to the zoo on Sunday also, and felt her toes curl thinking of how Alex had kissed her in the lion's house and she had been amused thinking he was stalking her like a lion.

She shook her head and was just trying to think up an answer when Katie said, "See what I mean? You're not even listening to me, Mom! What's up with that?"

She shrugged. "That's for me to know. There are some things even a Mom likes to keep to herself. We *are* allowed to have some privacy, you know. You keep yelling at me to remember that *you* need your space. Well, I need mine, too. So let's just get dinner on the table, so you guys have time for your showers before bedtime."

That had mollified Katie temporarily, but the look on her face had been contemplative and Tegan realized she was going to have to be very careful *not* to let Katie guess what was going on. No talking to Patti when the kids were home, and most definitely no late-night phone calls with Alex. She sighed as she glanced at the calendar and mentally counted the days until she could see him again. Then she reapplied herself to the job of being the best mother she knew how to be.

Twenty

Somehow they both got through the four weeks of waiting until the next Friday John was to come to pick up the children. The phone rang while the kids were at school, and Tegan had raced down the stairs from where she had been putting their laundry into their rooms, in order to grab the phone before the machine picked it up.

"Hello?" she panted into the phone.

There was a momentary silence, then in his low voice Alexander said, "I hope I'm not interrupting anything important?"

"Don't be silly," she worked on catching her breath. "I just ran down the stairs because I was up in the kids' rooms putting their laundry away. What, do you think I'm *doing* the mailman? Because if you know how anyone can get to him, Patti and some of the other neighborhood women would *love* to know!"

There was a low chuckle. "But, not you?"

She smiled. "No. I'm not in the market for a new man at this time, thank you. I have one that I'm very happy with, for now. But he's a little bit possessive, so I'm keeping an open mind about the whole thing. You could give me your number, so I could keep it just in case."

"Touché," Alex said. "I just called to tell you that you will need one night's formal clothes, since I'm taking you out to dinner, then to a ballet and you need to dress accordingly. The other night we will spend naked, of course, at my place. I liked the balance of our last weekend, and hope it will allow for us to once again enjoy each other's company to the utmost."

"Okay, I'll see what I can find in my closet. I haven't really had much need for anything other than jeans and sweatpants... you know us soccer moms. But I'll look through some of my stuff from before I had kids. That might work."

"You fit into clothes from before you had kids?" Alex was genuinely shocked.

"Yeah, why? Have you been talking to other women who have kids, in the four weeks since our last weekend together?"

Now it was Alex's turn to chide her. "Jealous?"

She snorted, then Alex laughed. "I had dinner at my parents' house, and my sister Julia moved back in with her three kids after her divorce last year. She spent a lot of time complaining about how she can't fit into any of her clothes from B.C."

"Yeah, before children, I know all about that," Tegan said. "I worked very hard, dieting and exercising like a madwoman after Kevin was born, to get down close to the same weight I started with. Then I realized it had all changed places, and what used to be up on top was now on the bottom, and my ribs looked weird and opened, and my hips had spread."

When he clucked sympathetically, she said, "The human race is really lucky women are the ones to have children, you know. If you men did it, we'd all be only children! You'd realize it hurts, and screws up your body, and none of you would do it more than once."

"You're not trying to pick a fight with me over the phone, are you?" he asked her, greatly amused.

"*No!*" she responded quickly. "Just making an observation."

"Good," he continued. "Since I'd rather fight with you in person. Then the making up part is that much more fun."

There was a silence for half a heartbeat, while they both contemplated just what kind of fun that would involve.

Then Alexander cleared his throat. "How about I pick you up at the commuter lot this time? I don't like the idea of you taking the el downtown by yourself at night."

"I'm a big girl and I can take care of myself," Tegan began, but Alex interrupted her.

"I know that, but there's also a little Mexican restaurant I know out by the airport. Some of my cousins still do baggage handling out at O'Hare, so they know all the good places to eat. I figure I will call from the parking lot, then we can pick something up there and bring it back here to eat."

"So I don't need to *wear* the fancy clothes, just bring them?"

"That's right. That's for Saturday night. I'm not sure I could keep my hands off you long enough to take you anywhere on Friday night. I had a hard enough time the last time we did it that way. Now that I *know* what I'm going to be getting once I have you here and naked, I don't want to torture myself by taking you out until I've had a chance to knock the edge off my hunger for you."

Tegan felt her bones melt and her panties pool with desire.

"Tegan, are you still there?" Alexander asked.

She sighed. "Yes. But my brain is filled with all of these ideas of positions we haven't tried yet, and I'm practically sliding off my chair with excitement. You really know how to get to me, don't you?"

He chuckled. "I hope so. Because you have certainly gotten under *my* skin. You're like an itch I can't reach myself. If I keep on talking to you about this, I'm not going to be able to finish the rest of my workday, so I'd better hang up now and let you get to your packing."

"Okay. John will get the kids after school again, so I can be out at the commuter lot by about six. That gives me time to pack and drive through the Friday afternoon traffic."

"Six o'clock it is. See you then."

"Bye, Alex."

They hung up, then both looked at the phones in their hands and sighed. "Five more hours."

Twenty-One

If John noticed anything different about the way Tegan was acting when he arrived to pick up their kids, he didn't say anything. Kevin was oblivious to anything but the excitement of getting to play with the new computer games his dad's roommate, Bill, frequently brought home from his job at a game store. But Katie watched her closely, so Tegan tried to act as if she didn't have any plans for the weekend. Since she wasn't aware *how* she normally acted, it was difficult to know if she was succeeding or not.

When they were all packed into the car and pulling out of the driveway, Tegan yelled, "Have fun!" at the kids.

Katie leaned out of the passenger side window and said significantly, "Try to miss us this time, okay, Mom?"

Tegan smiled pleasantly and waved, trying to ignore the sudden look of surprise on John's face. Then they were gone and she hurried into the house to finish her packing.

Alexander was waiting at the commuter lot when Tegan pulled up. She waved, then drove to find a parking spot. He followed her car and stopped behind her so he could take her bag and put it into his backseat. She also had a garment bag, so he hung that up next to her bag. He grabbed her for a quick kiss that extended itself the minute they touched each other. Instantly they were both breathing heavily until she pushed him away.

"Let's get the money into the machine before they notice us making out in the parking lot, and use that as an excuse to tow me!" While she jumped out of his car to put the money into the machine, he got on his cell phone and ordered in rapid Spanish. When she got back into the car, he was finishing up their order, and even though she had taken Spanish all through high school, and for two years in college, she found it difficult to follow, since he spoke so quickly. She watched him, and once again found herself lost in admiration at how good-looking he was and how unlike her blond, surfer-boy ex-husband.

He must have felt her eyes on him, because he turned. "¡Adiós!", then he reached across the seat to tilt her face up for a kiss.

"What did you order?" she asked, to make conversation and take her mind off of her own yearnings.

"You'll see," he said. "My cousins took me to this place once. We drank way too much tequila that night... but I do remember the food was almost as good as my mom's. So, since she won't cook for us without giving me the third degree about who you are, and what my intentions are, I figure this is the next best thing."

She smiled, then he added. "Maybe some day I'll take you for a traditional dinner meal at my mom's house. But it can't be on a day I pick you up after not seeing you for a month. My mom would get really pissed if I jumped on you anywhere in her house."

"As well she should!" Tegan laughed. "I don't even want to think about my own kids having sex yet. They're still too young, but it's coming up sooner than I want it to."

Soon they were at the restaurant, and Alexander insisted she stay in the car because he didn't want to leave it outside unguarded, nor did he want to bring her inside with him. "I can't worry about my car and you at the same time!" he told her. "This is *not* the nicest section of town, so stay put and I'll be right out."

It had been a very long time since anyone had looked out for her like that, so Tegan settled back into the expensive leather seat and put in a blues CD she found in the console that she hadn't heard, and she waited.

Alexander returned within a few minutes, carrying two large bags. When she raised her eyebrows at him, he smiled. "It's going to be a long night. We have enough food here for multiple eatings. I'm not going to give you any long breaks from pleasuring me, so you'll just have to eat a little bit at a time."

Tegan felt a chill run down her spine. Then Alexander hit the road and drove so fast and skillfully that they were back at his building downtown quicker than she would have imagined possible.

Once in his apartment, Alexander put the food bags on the counter and turned to her. "The last one naked has to be on the bottom, at least for the first time! First one naked gets to pick how and where!"

Their clothes flew off, and in no time they were kissing, fondling, groping and panting, and their mutual desire for each other took over, and they only made it as far as the futon.

Twenty-two

The food was almost as good as Patti's, as Tegan pointed out to Alexander, who laughed and proposed a cook-off between Patti and his mother. They drank beer with their food, and spent some time chatting in the Jacuzzi while they drank their after-dinner coffee. After they dried themselves off, Alexander asked Tegan to get him a robe out of his closet while he made them some home-made sangria to go with the tapas they still had left. Surprised at his desire to wear anything while they were together, she went over to open his closet and was shocked to see a teal silk nightgown hanging on the front hanger, with his robe on top of it. She looked closely at it, and was delighted to realize it was her size... the fabric was softer than anything she had ever felt. She slipped it on, then carried the robe with her into the kitchen to find Alexander had put on a Santana CD and was unconsciously dancing around while he sliced the fruit for the sangria he had already mixed up in a big glass pitcher.

He stopped what he was doing when she got to the doorway and stared at her. "It matches your eyes," he said softly. "I knew it would. Turn around, so I can admire it from all sides."

She handed him the black silk robe and he absent-mindedly slipped it on, leaving it open. She turned around, letting him see how the silk reflected the light, accentuating her curves. Her nipples poked through the front of the gown, and it was low-cut enough for her to have cleavage even without a bra. The gown was cut even lower in the back, so she had cleavage back there as well. She felt herself getting so turned on that she actually felt herself leaking her excitement down her legs. For his part, Alexander had an erection of mammoth proportions that stuck out the front of his open robe.

Seeking to reduce the tension filling the room, Tegan said, "Put down that knife! I don't want you to slip up and hurt yourself, now that there's no blood left in your brain."

He obediently put the knife down, then turned and poured some sangria into each of two wine glasses, handing one to her.

"To the most beautiful woman I have ever had the honor of paying homage to with my unworthy gifts."

She smiled self-consciously at him, clinked her glass against his, then took a drink. "Wow! This is really good!"

He smiled at her, his eyes blackened with passion. "Now, we do the dance of love... *now* we cha-cha."

As they danced, Tegan realized for the first time in her life, just *why* it was called the dance of love. The movements only increased their desires and she found it increasingly hard to continue dancing. She told him as much, panting while she spoke, and his eyes smoldered as he answered her.

"That's why we are dancing *here*, in my place. I don't dare try to do this with you in public anywhere. We'd be arrested."

They spent the rest of the evening dancing, drinking and making luxurious love on all of the available pieces of furniture in his living room. Afterwards, when they tumbled into his bed, unable to stay awake a moment longer, Alexander cradled Tegan in his arms. "I don't sleep as well without you next to me. I want to hold you, so that even in my sleep, I know you are here with me."

Her last thought before she fell asleep, was, "It would be so easy to fall in love with you, my Hispanic lover. I'm already half-way there." And instead of being terrified, she smiled as she drifted off to sleep, surrounded by the smell of Alex.

Twenty-three

Thanksgiving was the Thursday after their third weekend together. Since Tegan's family was back in Minnesota and Patti had come from New York, they had begun a tradition of their own in previous years when both of them were married. They had their dinner at Patti's house. She tried new recipes every year, incorporating the theme of turkey, but experimenting with new ways to spice up what was traditionally a fairly bland dinner. Some years were a big hit; some years were better left unremembered. But they were always happy affairs, with food enough for everyone to find something they liked, and after-dinner games enjoyed by all.

This year John had called Tegan and asked if he could join them for Thanksgiving dinner. Bill was going to be out of town visiting his own family for the first time in years. He was anxious about being invited back at all, so he had asked John to not be offended if he wasn't asked to go along. Since John's own family was currently not speaking to him, he had nowhere else to go. Tegan had reluctantly agreed, then called Patti to let her know.

"What the hell!" she cursed into the phone in her office, after the kids were in bed, presumably asleep. "Just because his boy-toy can't be with him, he has to horn in on *our* party?"

Patti sighed. "Oh well, it's not like we have to put up with the boy-toy also, or have both of our exes here at the same time. Mine will be with his current bimbo-du-jour, no doubt drinking up a storm somewhere. More power to him. I hope she dumps his ass and he's all broken up about it around Christmas. That would serve him right, the asshole."

Realizing Patti had just talked to her ex-husband, and was thus not terribly sympathetic at the moment, Tegan resigned herself to having to put up with the awkwardness of having her ex-husband eating a family meal with them, when he was most definitely *not* part of *her* family anymore. Katie and Kevin would be ecstatic about having their father join them for Thanksgiving, so Tegan accepted the inevitable and called him back to let him know they were to be at Patti's house by three, so there would be time for him to watch some football with the boys before dinner.

Twenty-four

Alexander got the call about the dinner from Edgar on the Monday after he had spent the weekend giving and receiving extreme pleasure from Tegan. He was told that Juanita had offered to host Thanksgiving this year, and their *madre* had gratefully agreed, since this way she only had to make the tamales and not the entire meal. Edgar asked him to bring the wine for the meal, and said their youngest brother, Roberto, would be bringing the beer. Alexander was pleased to hear that Roberto had been invited, so he quickly agreed to bring what was asked of him and was told to arrive about three, to have time to watch some football with his brothers and his dad.

With his usual punctuality, just before three on Thursday, he slowly drove down the street that his brother's family lived on... and just incidentally, also the woman of his wet dreams. He knew she lived only a couple of houses away from Edgar and Juanita, but had no idea which house was hers, so he drove slowly in order to look for a sign of where she lived. When he recognized the car in the driveway, he felt his heart skip a beat and he slowed down even further and made the split second decision to park right in front of her house.

"After all," he reasoned, "my elderly parents have to park in Edgar's driveway, and Julia has all of those kids. Roberto will be taking the train out here, but I should park out on the street."

He slowly got out of his car and spent some time looking around the neighborhood, as if he hadn't been there so many times before. But he hadn't... at least not since he had begun an affair with the woman who lived in the house he had parked in front of. He hoped for a glimpse of her, but was disappointed that she didn't appear to be home. So he slowly walked over to Edgar's house and let himself in through the open front door. Immediately he was assailed by his nieces and nephews, and he felt his tension relax, as he became *Tío Alejandro* once again.

Tegan looked out of her front window when she heard the car pull up, thinking it was John and wondering why he didn't just park in the driveway, since he knew she wouldn't be needing her car to get where they were eating. Patti only lived a block away. She saw the car and almost stopped breathing. When Alexander got out and looked around, she shrank behind her drapes, praying he didn't see her looking at him through the window. She watched his every move, when he began to walk towards Juanita's house, breathless from the excitement of seeing how confidently he carried himself, as if the whole world owed him everything and he just might deign to accept it.

"He's so gorgeous, and he's mine!" she thought, then she corrected herself with the reminder that theirs was merely a physical relationship, based on one weekend a month of world-rocking sex... no more, no less. And they'd had only had three weekends together. Certainly nothing to indicate she had any claim on him other than they had the hots for each other, in a big way.

She saw John's car pull up and park in the driveway, and she hurried back into the kitchen in order to finish up the relish dip that

Patti had given her the recipe for and requested she bring. The deal between them was Patti did all of the cooking, and she supplied the drinks. Then they figured out how to equally divide the cost, and she paid accordingly. But if Patti found a recipe that didn't appear to be too difficult for her best friend to attempt, she gave her a copy of it, and they both acted as if it was a huge surprise she was bringing anything at all to the dinner.

John rang the doorbell, and she heard the thunder of feet as their children raced to be the one to open the door for their dad. They were both excited and pleased he was coming to dinner with them, though Katie had watched Tegan closely when she was told he'd be there, for any reaction from her mom. Tegan, for her part, was determined to stay neutral for the day, in order for there to not be any awkwardness or unpleasantness. The added tension of knowing Alexander was comfortably ensconced only two houses away from her, made her hyper-aware of herself and she was glad she had bought an extra bottle of the white wine, *gewürztraminer*, that they all enjoyed with turkey every year.

"At this point, I'll probably drink one whole bottle myself," she thought, before she had to go through the motions of being polite to her ex-husband in front of their children. They collected all they were expected to bring along to Patti's house, and headed for the driveway. Tegan locked up the house and they walked together, as they had done for many years, down the block to her best friend's house for their traditional family celebration.

"Just like old times, huh?" asked John, while the kids walked ahead of them, excited about being together as a family again.

Tegan made a face at him, saying, "Yeah, but with one subtle difference. You're not going to be coming back to the house with us afterwards. Remember that."

John looked wounded, "But it's still nice, isn't it? Being together again, even if just for a short time?"

Tegan regarded him with distaste for a quick moment, before catching sight of Katie looking back at them, "Just don't get too comfortable 'in the moment.' I'm only being polite to you for their sakes. Stay away from me once I start drinking, or I may say something we'll both regret."

John started to say something, but Tegan hurried to catch up with their kids and the moment was lost.

Twenty-five

Alexander felt like he was choking on his own jealousy. He watched through the window next to the chair that he had seated himself on, as Tegan walked along in front of the house he was in and didn't even look to see if he was there. She must know he was… his car was right in front of her house! And just who the hell was that man who was walking right beside her, as if he belonged there? The only man who belonged next to her was him. He felt his hand clenching around the beer he held, and forced himself to relax before he broke the bottle in his fist.

Edgar noticed he was looking out of the window and yelled to his wife, "Hey, there's John, going to dinner at Patti's with Tegan and the kids. Will miracles never cease?"

Juanita stepped into the living room and took a quick look out the window, saying, "I'll have to call her tomorrow and ask what kind of blackmail he used on her to get her to let him go with her to the dinner."

"Blackmail?" Alexander forgot he was trying to appear nonchalant, and asked in spite of himself.

Edgar laughed. "Yeah, they got divorced a couple of years ago. Too bad, they were a nice couple. They look really good together, though, don't they? And they made a couple of nice-looking kids.

Rosa baby-sits for them sometimes and Katie sometimes helps Rosa with our kids, when we leave her alone with all of them." Juanita poked her head back into the room, saying, "I think you should be opening the wine now, Edgar; I'm going to be taking the turkey out of the oven, and you need to be there to be sure it's done."

Edgar and Juanita went back into the kitchen together, and Alexander continued to watch Tegan's adorable butt as she walked with her family to the corner. Then they turned to cross the street and passed out of his line of vision.

He spent the rest of the day in a jealous fit, trying not to let it affect how he interacted with his family, but thinking only of the fact that there was another man with Tegan, with *his* woman, spending the day relaxing with their kids... the kids they had to have had sex with each other to create. He knew she would never have allowed *him* to spend the day with her, since he was not allowed to be near her kids. He was good enough for her to strip naked with and scream herself hoarse with, but not for her to offer to share any other part of her life with.

He should have stopped himself from drinking the moment he realized he was brooding about this jealousy of his, but he didn't. His youngest brother, Roberto, was the one to realize what was happening to him, what he was doing to himself, though Roberto didn't understand why. So when he got obnoxious after dinner, Roberto took him outside and sat with him on the porch, while he silently brooded. Then he brought his oldest brother coffee until he sobered up enough to be able to talk again.

"I've fallen in love with a woman who only wants me for sex, once a month," he told Roberto. Then he stopped short, realizing what he had just said out loud, and realizing for the first time, he had drunk way too much before and during dinner and he was going to catch hell from his *madre* for this day.

He was not surprised when Roberto looked truly puzzled at him, saying, "But I thought you only chase women for that one thing: to have sex with them. Then, when they are no longer a challenge to you, you drop them like a hot potato. Why is this one any different?"

"Why, indeed?" he asked himself, through his drunken fog. Then he had a blinding flash of insight into his own personality, and he was struck dumb by the revelation. He wanted her *because* she wouldn't let him have anymore than she was willing to give him. If she told him she loved him, he'd probably get bored with her, as had happened so many times before now. But she had established the limits, and like the alpha-male he was, he was chafing under the restrictions that kept him from claiming her as his own, in front of everyone.

But what would that accomplish? Would he be able to step up and accept being a permanent part of her life, or would he start looking around for another challenge? Alexander wasn't sure what he felt about himself, but he was pretty sure disgust was part of it.

One thing was certain: he wanted Tegan with a desire bordering on obsession. But was he up for the challenge of becoming an integral part of her life, or was he just over-reacting to the line in the sand she had drawn, letting him have only so much of her and not a smidgeon more? He groaned as he put his head into his hands. He had no idea what the answer was, nor did he have any idea how to find out. And the fact he was a forty-two year old man, who had behaved abominably at a family dinner because he was having a midlife crisis over a woman, was unbearably embarrassing.

He gratefully accepted the cups of coffee Roberto brought him, as he attempted to make some sense out of his situation. When his brother offered to drive him home, he took him up on his offer.

"You've always been there for me," Roberto reminded him. "I'm just grateful to be able to repay you in any small way for what you mean to me."

Since they both knew what Roberto meant, Alexander accepted his brother's idea of repayment for past support. Tegan's house was still dark when they left, but that was just as well. Alexander was feeling too out-of-control to have been able to meet her ex-husband on the street, without feeling the need to exert his physical strength over him, to show Tegan that *he* was the better man for her. Since he knew brute physical strength rarely, if ever, impressed women, and especially an intelligent woman like Tegan, he was glad to leave before she and her family reappeared close to his car.

When his brother got him to his condo, Roberto offered to stay and drink with him for a while, if he needed to talk to someone. But Alexander declined that offer because he wanted to be alone with his thoughts. He wasn't sure he even wanted to face his thoughts himself, much less share them with someone who had idolized him throughout their childhood. Once he was alone, Alexander stripped down to his shorts, sat in front of his fireplace and thought long and hard about what his life had become and what he wanted it to be. He passed out on the futon and didn't move into his bed until the next morning, when he took a few aspirin to kill his hang-over and went back to bed to brood.

Twenty-six

For her part, Tegan didn't enjoy Thanksgiving, either. The knowledge that Alexander was two houses away from her house, but she couldn't see him or talk to him, drove her crazy. Once she got to Patti's house and opened the wine, she kept at it until both bottles were gone; then she went into Patti's private stock and opened one of those bottles as well. She was rude to John and brusque to the children. She was totally out of control, and only Patti had any idea why she was acting like that, and even she was unable to stop what appeared to be inevitable.

In the middle of an argument with John, when it appeared she was about to blurt out *why* he had left her, Patti hustled her into the next room and pushed Tegan onto her bed. "I don't know what's with you tonight, girl, but you need to pass out before you say things you don't want the kids to hear!"

At that, Tegan started to cry, telling Patti she was terrified she might be falling in love with a man who only wanted her for monthly sex. Patti had to push her fist into her mouth in order not to laugh at her drunken friend. She herself would have given her left boob for a man who wanted her for sex... even if that was all he ever offered! A simple, uncomplicated relationship. What a pleasant change from what they had both been through. But she acted like a loyal friend, and calmed Tegan down, made her drink a couple of big glasses of water, then tucked her into her own bed and turned out the light. Before she even closed the door, Tegan was snoring. Patti went back into the kitchen to do the dishes and watch John keep the kids amused with a tournament of video games. He offered to stay the night at his old house with his kids, but Patti knew Tegan wouldn't approve, so she hustled him out the door and told him to go home, after the girls yawned themselves into going to bed and the boys showed signs of being too tired to keep on playing.

She poured herself a large glass of wine from her secret stock Tegan had broken into, and watched the moon travel across the sky while toasting the errant night spirits who had bewitched her friend. She prayed to the good ones to kick some sense into her head in the morning. Eventually, she fell asleep on the couch in her own living room, amused by their rendition of a family celebration, and inordinately grateful her own ex-husband had had the good taste not to appear at her door.

Twenty-seven

Alexander called the Friday before the week of Christmas, because it had been a month since he had last seen Tegan, and he was anxious to tell her his plans for the weekend. Since he called during the day, once again she was able to talk to him without worrying about being overheard.

"So, when can I pick you up from the commuter parking lot tonight?"

"I'm sorry, Alex, but you can't. The holidays change everything for visitation purposes. I should have told you this earlier, but when I'm with you, I can't think well enough to make coherent words come out of my mouth. I'm too busy screaming."

Trying not to yell out his disappointment into the phone, Alexander tried to modulate his voice. "So, what does this mean for us?"

"Well, John got the kids last year for Christmas week, and I had them for New Year's week. This year is the opposite. I'll have them all next week, so I'm taking them to visit my parents in Minnesota. They haven't seen them for a long time. Everyone is looking forward to it."

"I'm not," Alexander noted dryly.

Tegan sighed. "Actually, I'm not looking forward to it as much as I should. Not only is Katie being even more difficult than usual, but I will miss you. You're not the only one who is disappointed this won't be a fun weekend for us. I love to drive, but doing the whole nine hours or so that it takes me to get up there by myself is kind of tiring. But the plans are made, so that's that."

Alexander cleared his throat. "Can I take that to mean you will be free of your children for the whole following week?"

"Not the whole week. I'm leaving with the kids this Sunday, and I will be coming back next Sunday. So John will pick them up on Monday morning, and then bring them back the following Sunday at dinnertime, as usual. The kids are thrilled at getting to have multiple Christmas celebrations, so I'm trying to be excited for their sakes."

Alexander felt his pulse beginning to race at the idea of having her to himself for almost an entire week. "Does this mean that I can pick you up on Monday and have you to myself for the rest of the week?"

There was a silence, during which they both entertained themselves with visions of what they could do with that much time alone together.

In a breathy voice, Tegan said, "I suppose so. If you don't mind leaving me alone in your apartment while you go to work all day."

"I have a better idea. I think I'll take the whole week after Christmas off, since I haven't taken any vacation time all year. Most of my clients will be working only sporadically, at best, so it's a good time for a holiday for me, too. Would that be agreeable to you, or do you really want to be alone in my condo during the day?"

Tegan laughed softly. "Have the chance to have you for almost seven whole days, naked for most of the time, with no interruptions? Gosh, I'll have to think about it. Okay, I've thought about it long enough. *Yes!* Oh, my God, *yes!*"

Once again, Tegan was sure she could hear him smiling into his phone.

"Tegan, my love, your exuberance is most gratifying. But I really prefer screaming and moaning the best. So now I guess I'll have to cancel the plans I made for this weekend and get to work planning our week after Christmas. Why don't you call me at my condo on that Monday after your kids have left, so I can tell you what to pack? I'll have all of the plans in place by then."

"Okay," she said, already distracted by imagining so many days of unadulterated pleasure.

"And since I'm going to be worried about you driving all of that way alone, please give me a call on Sunday night to let me know you have arrived safely. I don't care how late you call... I'll be awake waiting to hear from you. Wait until everyone in the house is asleep, if you have to. But call me, okay?"

Now it was Tegan's turn to smile into her phone. "All right, if you insist."

"I do. And also, I think I will send a cab to get you on that Monday, so we don't have to keep driving to the commuter lot once a day to safeguard your car. We can have the cab drive you to the commuter lot, then I'll pick you up from there. That way there's no way the cab driver can tell anyone where you were going. Does that suit your sense of secrecy?"

There was a note of unhappiness in that last line, and Tegan wasn't sure what to make of that. She decided to just ignore it.

"Okay, I'll finish packing when you call, then wait for the cab to get here. But you have to let me pay for the cab fare, at least."

Alexander sighed heavily. "If you insist. But that will be the last money you will need for the week. The rest is my Christmas treat to you."

Tegan giggled. "Need I ask what you want me to give you?"

Alexander dropped his voice even lower. "You *know* what I like. Just put a big bow on it, and I'll be happy."

Tegan said, "Oh crap! There's another call coming in on my other line. It's probably my mother... she's been calling me twice a day telling me what to bring, asking me what to cook, etc., etc. I'm going to have to pick it up. I guess I'll talk to you late on Sunday night, okay?"

"Okay. Until then. And Tegan?"

"What?"

"Merry Christmas."

"Merry Christmas to you too, Alex. Bye."

Twenty-eight

Alexander sat staring at the phone for a while. He had other calls coming in, too, but he ignored them. His disappointment at having their weekend postponed was tempered with the knowledge he would have a whole week alone with Tegan to try to convince her he was ready for their relationship to progress to the next level. He was ready to get to know her kids. He was ready to openly date her, so his family and hers both knew what was happening to them. And the fact was that even though he had only known her for about three months, he was seriously considering... what... asking her to marry him? That was certainly a possibility, but one still too far off in the future for him to worry about now.

What he had to worry about was talking to the boss about taking off the week after Christmas. Then he had some calls to make to set up a week for them both to remember. He smiled again. Damn! He was getting used to smiling since he had met her. He had to watch himself, or he was going to stop being feared at work. He scowled, then shrugged. "Nope, not in the mood for scowling right now." He unhooked himself from his telephone equipment, and got up to go talk to his boss.

That night, Alexander spent some time online, making last-minute reservations for a two-day, two-night stay for the weekend after New

Year's at a cabin in the White Pines state park in rural Oregon, Illinois. They would be able to head out the day after New Year's Day and stay through Sunday morning. He was picking Tegan up Monday morning, and they would stay at his condo for the first few nights, since New Year's Eve was on a Wednesday... he thought about sitting naked on the balcony, watching the fireworks with her, then making fireworks of their own afterwards. Trying to distract himself from that line of thought, and wanting to avoid sharing her with crowds this time, he also checked out a menu, then e-mailed a request for room service to cook for them on New Year's Eve, ordering a filet mignon steak dinner for two, complete with chocolate-drizzled cream puffs for dessert. The idea of smearing the whipped cream from the cream puffs all over Tegan's various body parts, then licking them off, made him break out into a cold sweat.

He was debating taking his shower early when the phone rang.

"Hello?"

"*Hola, mi hermano.*"

"Edgar?"

"*Sí*"

"Why the *español*?"

Edgar laughed, "*Lo siento!* Sorry! I just got off the phone with *madrecita*, and since we were talking about what she wants me to pick up for her to give to the kids for Christmas, we were speaking Spanish."

Alexander chuckled, "Haven't you and Juanita taught them any Spanish yet?"

"Not much, when there's always a need to say things in front of them they can't understand. Rosa has picked up a lot, plus she's taking it in high school. The worst part of *that* is she corrects our grammar sometimes. She calls what we speak ghetto *español*."

Alexander laughed. "Well, considering where and how we lived when we were growing up, she's not that far off, bro'!"

"So, what I called about was, do you want to come over for dinner tomorrow night? I know you had told me you had other plans, but Roberto is coming over, and he wants to bring a friend over to meet us. 'Nita and I thought it might be less awkward if you were here, too. If you have a date, you could bring her, too. That way there would be two of them to get to know at once."

"No, my date has been postponed. But I could make it for dinner. What time do you want me to get there?"

"What about coming over around four? 'Nita and I should be home from Christmas shopping by then, and we can have some brother-to-brother time before dinner."

"Uh-oh, am I in trouble?"

"No, but I'm still wondering what put that bug up your ass on Thanksgiving. Maybe if I get you alone, you'll tell me what's going on in your life these days. And I don't mean with your job. There's something else going on, and if you can't tell your own brother about it, who can you talk to?"

"Maybe I don't want to tell anyone about it just yet, little brother. But I'll bring some beer with me, and we'll see."

"Okay. *Adios!*"

Alexander shook his head at the phone once he hung up. "Not yet, little brother, not yet. But soon, once I get her to agree, then everyone will know."

And once again, Alexander felt himself smiling.

Twenty-nine

"Murphy's Law rules!" Tegan thought, "Everything that can go wrong, is going wrong."

She had been rushing around for two days trying to get everything packed, wrapped and ready to drive up to Minnesota. First Katie's favorite shirt had disappeared, and she burst into tears and refused to go at all unless it was found, washed and folded up into her duffle bag. Then Kevin's game-boy picked that week to implode, so he had screamed he couldn't possibly ride forever in a car with his bratty sister, unless he had a new game-boy. Then she got a flat tire on the way to do some last-minute Christmas shopping, and had to get that fixed at a station, while she worried about the kids being home alone until she got home, well after dark on Friday.

The shirt was found, stuffed into the back of one of Katie's drawers. Patti's son Jake loaned Kevin his game-boy, since Patti had reminded Jake he wouldn't need it as they weren't going anywhere over the holidays. The tire had been fixed, and the boys were now over at Patti's house, doing… what else …playing video games on a snowy Saturday afternoon. So when Rosa called and asked if Katie could come over to help her sit for her siblings, their parents being in the city doing some shopping of their own, Tegan was glad to say yes in order to get the house to herself. Since she was the queen of order, she found it immensely irritating when things were not going as planned and she needed some alone time to rearrange her karma.

Once Katie was gone, Tegan took a deep breath and got to work on making her life easier. At least the parts she could control.

Thirty

As usual, since Alexander prided himself on his punctuality, at five minutes to four he arrived at Edgar's house. He thought about parking in front of Tegan's house again, but remembering the last time he had, he figured it might be a bad idea to tempt fate, so he parked in front of Edgar's house. He still looked hopefully towards her house, but despite the car being in the driveway, there was no sign of her. He sighed, grabbed the beer out of his car and went into Edgar's house through the always-open door.

The only one in sight was the youngest baby, sitting in a door swing and babbling to herself. He yelled, "Hello?" The baby smiled and burbled.

A young, blond girl who looked strangely familiar came bustling into the room, carrying a baby bottle she was testing on her arm. She stopped short when she saw him.

"Who are you?" she asked, moving protectively over to the baby, who was holding out her arms to the girl, trying to grab for the bottle.

"I'm *Tío Alejandro*, and that baby is my youngest niece, though I forget what her name is, since there's so many of them in this house. And who are you, young lady?"

She smiled at him and once he saw her dimples, he knew where he had seen her before.

"I'm Katie. I live a couple of houses down from here. Rosa has been sitting for me and my brother... oops! I mean, for my brother and me, for years. So when she needs help taking care of all the kids, she calls me. I just turned twelve, so I'm old enough now. She says she is training me to take over her baby-sitting business, for when she starts dating."

She looked stricken and looked around the room saying in a quieter, conspiratorial voice, "You won't tell her parents I told you, right? They keep telling her she can't date until she's eighteen and moved out of the house. But there's this guy she likes, and they're not supposed to know about it. She'll kill me if she knows I told you."

Alexander smiled at Tegan's daughter. "Your secret is safe with me, Miss Katie. Just ask Rosa. I already know about the boy she likes. Sometimes there are things you need to tell a grown-up, but it can't be your parents. That's what uncles are for. Trust me... I have lots of nieces and nephews. I'm the oldest of nine kids and most of my brothers and sisters are married and popping out children right, left and center."

Katie smiled at him, as she expertly took the baby out of the swing and settled down on the couch with her, holding the bottle for her. "She likes it if you let her think she's holding it herself," she explained to him, as he sat down on the couch across from her and opened a beer.

Just then Rosa came into the room looking exasperated. She smiled at Alexander and ran over to give him a hug. *"Tío Alejandro!* I'm so happy to see you! We need all of the hands we can get around here. I just got a phone call from Mom, and they are stuck in traffic because there's an accident on the highway. They don't know when they'll be home. They asked if you were here yet, but I told them no. They said they would call back soon to give me an update. I've got dinner in the oven, but I've got to get back to the girls who are having a major fight upstairs over their dolls. The boys are downstairs playing video games. Katie, thanks so much for giving the baby her bottle. If you can get her down for a nap, that would be one less to worry about."

There was a crash and a squeal from upstairs, and Rosa rolled her eyes. "Sounds like I better get back up there." Then she ran up the stairs, two at a time.

Alexander smiled at Katie, "This is what it was like growing up in my house, too. Mass pandemonium all of the time. But my grandparents were always around to give a hand, so we managed okay."

Katie shook her head, "It's not like this in my house. My brother never talks to me anymore, and my mom is acting all weird lately. She got really depressed after the divorce, but she's been acting different now, and I can't figure out what's wrong with her. We're going up to see her parents in Minnesota for Christmas week leaving tomorrow, so I'm hoping she calms down enough to talk about what's on her mind, maybe sometime during the long drive out there?"

Alexander wondered if Tegan was aware of how much her daughter was figuring out on her own. He also wanted to tell her about his relationship with her mom, but realized that was not his secret to tell. So he changed the subject.

"Your parents are divorced? That must have been hard on you and your brother."

She shrugged, "For a while, it was. But now we get to live in two places, and celebrate the holidays twice, once with Mom and once with Dad. So it's not so bad. I'd still like it better if they got back together, but it's beginning to look like that's not going to happen, because I don't think Mom even likes him anymore. She never says anything bad about him to me, but she's hardly polite to him and she won't let him bring his roommate over to pick us up. So even though Kevin really likes him because he brings new video games home from his job all the time, Mom won't let Bill come to our house at all. What's up with that?"

Alexander felt as if he had been struck. He carefully maintained a neutral face and cleared his throat, then asked, "Does your dad live in an apartment near here?"

"No, it's in the city."

"I live in the city. In fact, I'm downtown, near the Lincoln Park Zoo. Which is really handy, since I like to go there all of the time. It helps me to think while I'm looking at the animals."

Katie burped the baby, then put her back on her lap to give her the rest of the bottle.

"Well, Dad's place is further up the lake. Up Clark Street for a while. I heard him once telling Mom his neighborhood is called boys town and she yelled at him, but they closed the door and I didn't hear what they were arguing about."

Alexander tried to focus on talking with the girl, but his mind was racing and his heart was aching for Tegan. He wanted to run over to her house and wrap her in his arms and tell her he now knew why she was so skittish about trusting men, and why she was keeping him at arm's length. He wanted to hold her and to assure her he would *never* hurt her like her ex-husband had; that not only would he never leave her for a man, he was beginning to be certain he would never leave her for another woman either.

The baby had fallen asleep on Katie's lap, and she smiled up at him, her dimples making him feel even more keenly how much he missed her mother.

"I like to go to the zoo a lot, too," Katie told him in a quieter tone, so as not to wake the baby. "My favorite animal is the lion, since he's the king of the jungle. I really like to go the lion's house and sit and watch them. Life would be so much simpler if I was a lion. It's so much easier to go from being a lion cub to being a grown-up lion. If I could pick, that's what I would be. They never get acne. They never have boys slam them into lockers. They never worry they won't ever get big boobs, or no boys will ever ask them out on a date. They never have to do homework. And they never have to worry about their mom, wondering if she's going to flip out someday because she never lets herself relax."

She sighed heavily, and Alexander realized he should say something, but he couldn't for the life of him think of what would help her feel better.

"But lion's don't ever fall in love, either," he observed, "and that's one of the very best things about being a human. It can hurt, but it can be wonderful, too. There's so much for you to look forward to, Katie. You are a beautiful girl, and intelligent and thoughtful. You will someday have to beat boys off with a stick, because they will *all* want to date you, whether you grow big boobs or not. And remember, I know a lot about these things. I'm an uncle to lots and lots of kids."

Katie smiled at him, flashing him her dimples again. "My mom only has a sister and she lives in Minnesota. Will you be *my* uncle, too?"

He felt himself melt with feelings for this young girl who reminded him so much of her mother. He smiled back at her. "Of course, Katie. There's always room for one more kid in my life. You can call me *Tío Alejandro. Tío* means uncle in Spanish."

Suddenly there was shouting and the sounds of scuffling coming from downstairs, and Alexander realized it was time for him to actually earn his supper.

"Uh-oh! It sounds like the natives are getting restless down there. I'd better go insert my grown-up macho self in-between some of those boys, since my brother Edgar will kill me if he comes home to find they've broken each other's noses, like he and I did once."

123

Katie smiled at him. "Okay, I've got to go put the baby down for her nap. Then I'll check on the dinner and go help Rosa with the girls. Thanks for giving me someone to talk to while I fed the baby. And thanks for being my uncle, too."

As he went down the stairs, Alexander hoped he had found a way to neutralize Tegan's fears about protecting her children from him. But he realized it was not yet the right time to tell her that, so he tucked his conversation with Katie away in his brain to examine later. He also planned to spend some time later, figuring out how to let Tegan know what he had found out about her divorce, and to help her deal with what was obviously still causing her pain. Maybe then, she would be able to move on enough to let him have a larger part in her life.

Once downstairs, he got involved wrestling with a horde of wild nephews and there wasn't any more time to think while he worked on remembering how to protect himself from the sneak attacks his brothers all used to use on their oldest brother.

Thirty-one

Alexander waited up for Tegan's call on Sunday. Finally, the phone rang at about one in the morning. He quickly answered and was relieved to hear her voice.

"So you made it okay?" he asked her, stating the obvious.

"Yes. I made a few stops so we could all stretch our legs; I had forgotten what a long, boring drive it is. The kids were too jazzed up to sleep, so I had to wait until they were in bed, and then my parents wanted to stay up to chat for a while. They don't stay up very late anymore, though, since they're getting on in years."

"I miss you," Alexander said simply.

"I miss you, too," Tegan replied, with a small sigh. "I'm already looking forward to being able to spend a whole week with you. Have you made any plans for us yet?"

Alexander chuckled softly. "Yes, but you're not getting to hear about them until you call me next Monday morning. Suffice it to say, I think you'll be pleased."

"Okay, then. I guess I'll say good-night... and Merry Christmas again, Alex."

"Merry Christmas to you, honey, and see you soon."

~ * ~

Their week apart flew by, and at last it was Monday morning. Tegan waved to her kids as they drove away with their dad for their second Christmas celebration of the season. Katie had spent some time over the past week, trying to get her mom to talk about what was bothering her... what was causing her to be so pre-occupied lately. Tegan had managed to turn aside her daughter's concerns, but she was wondering how long it would be before she would be exposed to her kids as a wanton woman, who met a man just for sex on a monthly basis.

"Betcha they don't cover *that* in those stupid abstinence-based programs at their school," Tegan had said to Patti, while they chatted over the phone late Sunday night.

Once Alexander had told her where they were going for the weekend at the end of their week together, and to pack something to wear to try out cross-country skiing, she got really excited about the mini-vacation, and not just for the excellent sex she expected. Alexander said he had never tried cross-country skiing, and the fact he wanted to try new things with her, even out of bed, was a good sign their relationship might have a chance to grow. She packed hurriedly, since the cab was already on its way to her house. She had felt like a piece of cargo, being left at the commuter lot by the cabbie, then picked up by Alexander right after the cab left.

He had stowed her things in the trunk next to his and then given her a quick kiss. They got into his car and he drove them to his condo, where they unloaded her two duffle bags and got into the elevator up to his floor. Since it was traditional for him to grope her on the elevator, he didn't disappoint her. A few sweaty moments later, he picked her bags up off the floor and she tried to hold her blouse closed under her coat while he carried her things to his condo.

Once in his place, he turned to her, dropped her bags and she flew into his arms. Clothing was ripped off, as they both worked single-mindedly towards the same goal. Once they were almost naked, he surprised her by picking her up and carrying her, kissing her all the way, to his bedroom, and then he sat on his bed and lay back to let her have her way with him. She kissed him, licking and sucking on his tongue, then she trailed her tongue down his scratchy neck to his chest. She made wet circles on his chest, as she paid special attention to his sensitive nipples. She began to work her way down lower to his flat abdomen, then she licked at him through his now impossibly-tight briefs, and he moaned his impatience at her slow movements.

She smiled up at him. "You're not in a hurry, are you? After all, we have plenty of time, this time." She teased him by rubbing him, then leaning over to lick at him again, while he repeatedly lifted his butt off the bed, trying to get her to strip him.

Finally, she moved herself in-between his legs and carefully pulled his last vestige of clothing off. His rampant erection sprang into her face. She laughed, enjoying the power she felt over this strong man, as she grasped him at the root and lowered her mouth over him, hearing him gasp with pleasure. She devoured him, running wet kisses up and down the length of him, taking him in her mouth and swallowing hard. She repeated each movement, again and again, until he groaned and said, "No, Tegan, I want to be in you, in your sweet body."

He gently pulled her up and she quickly rolled the condom he handed her onto him, then put her thighs on either side of his hips, and eased herself down onto him. They both completely lost control, as she rolled her hips and felt herself spasm each time he thrust himself forward to come to the end of her. The position they were in made his thrusts so deep, there was no place else for him to go. Still he pushed himself into her, then withdrew slightly and pushed his hips forward again. She drew herself up, leaned backwards and he pulled at her nipples, rolling them between his fingers. Blasts of light played on the back of her eyelids, and she screamed out her pleasure, as over and over again he felt her muscles squeezing him while she quivered. With one last massive thrust of his hips, he pushed so far in she was sure she would taste him in her throat. He shouted incoherently, as he felt himself explode into her. Once again, her waves of pleasure combined with his and he knew it must be possible for men to have multiple orgasms, as he trembled and held tightly to the one woman who could take anything he wanted to give, multiply it and give it back to him. They both collapsed and were barely conscious, as they gasped for breath and felt their bodies quiver from the total release of tension.

"Wow!" Tegan whispered, when her breathing finally allowed her to speak again. She had collapsed on top of him and now she rolled to one side, as he tied off the condom, then wrapped her in his arms.

He smiled, as he picked his head up to kiss the top of hers, then fell back onto his pillow. "Wow is right! Just when I think it can't possibly get any better between us, it does. I don't know how it keeps happening, but I sincerely hope it continues."

She picked her head off of his chest to look him in the eye, "Aren't you afraid it might kill us?"

"Nah, we're both in good shape," he smiled mischievously at her, adding, "For our ages. Besides, what a way to go! The mortician would never be able to wipe the smile off of our faces."

She laughed. "If they couldn't separate us, they'd never find a coffin, or oven big enough to slide us both into!"

She rested her head on him and they lay content in each other's arms, enjoying the afterglow from their reunion.

Thirty-two

They were both quiet, enjoying the beauty of the fields covered in snow, as they drove to their cabin in the woods on Friday. Each was mentally reliving their favorite moments of the past few days, with time spent merely enjoying each other's company while talking, interspersed with passionate encounters that were off the Richter scale in making the earth move. Alex had shown her the list he had made of all of the pieces of his furniture they had already used in their lovemaking, and they had purposed involved all the rest, so he could truthfully say they had screwed on every surface he owned. The futon by the fireplace and the Jacuzzi were two of their favorites, as was the massive waterbed Tegan had taken to referring to as the gymnasium, for the amount of positions he had taken her in while on it.

On New Year's Eve, they had exchanged gifts and not surprisingly, most of them contributed to sexual enjoyment. She had given him two pairs of silk boxers, since she said she wanted to lick him through them, and they were classier than the gym shorts he usually wore when he had to answer the door to pay for their food deliveries.

He had given her a silk peignoir set, this one in black, since he liked the contrast with her white skin so much.

She had also given him two different scents of massage oil, and the massages she gave him were part of the gift, she explained. For his part, Alex had to admit to her that, as in strip clubs, he had always chafed at not being able to act on his erection when he was getting a massage. She laughed and told him as long as he got his massages from her, that wasn't a problem. He had turned the tables on her, and did such a thorough job relaxing her, she fell asleep in the middle of the afternoon.

He had taken that opportunity to do a quick check of the messages on his answering machine, and unexpectedly, was pleased there wasn't anything that couldn't be taken care of by someone else in his office or wait until the following Monday when he would be back at work. He had sat back in the chair in his office, feeling only a deep sense of contentment and happiness. No constant urges to drive himself to achieve, just peace and relaxation. He shook his head in wonderment, then went to lie down next to the woman who was responsible for this welcome change in him.

They had also given each other books: she had given him some best-sellers involving international intrigue, since she thought an alpha-man like him might enjoy reading about men as driven as he was.

He gave her a book of erotic short stories he insisted she read aloud to him, while he made their breakfast the next morning. They had both gotten so excited he burned the toast and the bacon was crunchy, but it didn't matter. Nothing bothered either one of them, as long as they were together.

New Year's Eve had been a wonderful night, even more so than usual. They had both worn their new silk lingerie and sipped champagne and danced to many different kinds of music while they waited for their dinner to be delivered. After they ate, they enjoyed some coffee and Alex fulfilled his fantasy of stripping Tegan naked and smearing the cream puff's whipped cream all over her, so he could lick it off. Not to be outdone, she did the same to his most sensitive body part, and they had nearly missed the fireworks, they were so involved with making explosions of their own.

Watching the city's celebration from his balcony, Tegan sighed with pleasure. "I can't remember the last time I was this happy. You really are spoiling me, you know. No other man will ever be able to match up to you. I guess when you get tired of me, I'll have to run away and join a nunnery."

Alexander had moved closer to her from behind and covered her with his body, running his hands down her arms, then leaning against her, feeling her warmth set him on fire again. "I don't think it's possible for me to get tired of you, Tegan, honey. The more I have you, the more I want you. It just gets better and better for us. So don't go filling out any applications for nunneries just yet, okay? Let's just see where this can take us."

She turned to face him, looking up into his dark eyes. "It can't take us anywhere, remember. There are limits to it, and as hard as it is, we have to stick to them. I'm protecting my children. That's more important to me than even the time I spend with you."

He lowered his head to snuggle her, sighing into her hair, "As you wish, Mistress. But let me know if you ever change your mind about that."

Then he claimed her lips once more, and they moved back onto the futon to get out of the cold, and to once again, make fireworks of their own.

Thirty-three

When they got to the cabins, Tegan was charmed with the place and wanted to go with Alexander into the office to check in. There was a restaurant as well as a gift shop. The woman who verified their reservation gave them their key. "And congratulations on your anniversary, Mr. and Mrs. Reyes. We are pleased you have decided to celebrate with us, and we hope you enjoy your stay."

Tegan raised her eyebrows at Alex, but he merely thanked the clerk and led Tegan out of the door to his car, so they could make the short drive over to their private cabin in the woods.

"Mr. and Mrs.? Anniversary? What's going on here?" Tegan demanded.

Alexander smiled guiltily at her. "It's a family-run place. They only allow married couples to make reservations. So it was only a little white lie."

When they got to the cabin, he opened the door, picked her up and carried her through the doorway. "And it *was* to have been our anniversary celebration. The timing is off because of your changing *when* we could be together. I'm just glad they let me change the dates."

He put her down and went out to the car to get their things. When he returned, he dropped them onto the nearest chair and locked the door. He turned to her, and waved his hands around at the room, "Nice, huh?"

Tegan walked over to him and looked up at him questioningly, "Anniversary of what?"

His eyes smoldered again as he lifted her face and looked deeply into her eyes, "We were supposed to be here together on Friday, the nineteenth of December. That would have been exactly three months since a certain woman I barely knew drove me so utterly insane with lust that I acted like an uncivilized animal and had my way with her without even asking her permission."

He lowered his head and kissed her, gently, then with increasing urgency. He moaned, then lifted his lips from hers to say, "I have been trying to get you out of my system ever since, but the more I have you, the more I want you. You've become an obsession with me, Tegan O'Neill. I have to have you."

With that, he pushed her backwards onto the bed and proceeded to have her again and again, in many different ways. By the time they were ready to leave the bed, it was getting dark out, and they were both hungry.

"Are we going out to eat?" Tegan asked.

"Not tonight, my dear," Alexander said with a smile. "Tomorrow night we can eat at the restaurant in the main office. We'll have breakfast there tomorrow morning, too. But tonight I have made other arrangements."

"What kind of arrangements?" she asked, thinking the town was a long drive away from where they were. It was a typical small town, so delivery choices would be limited.

Alexander pulled on his pants and his boots, tossed his coat over his naked torso, saying, "I'll be right back. Wait right here."

In a moment, he returned carrying a large box Tegan recognized as being one of Patti's containers for carrying food to parties. Alexander put the box down on the table by the kitchen area that held a tiny sink, a microwave, a small fridge and a coffeemaker. He went outside and returned carrying a second, smaller box. He put that one down and closed and locked the door again.

Tegan had been snuggling down under the covers, since it was so chilly outside. Now she got up and walked over to see what was in the boxes. She was surprised and pleased to see there was a microwavable tray of Patti's chili *rellenos*, as well as one of tamales; there were chips, with salsa and guacamole in smaller containers and there were plates to put it all on, and silverware.

She turned to Alexander and asked, "When did you get this all set up?"

He smiled back. "I called Patti last week, while you were gone. She delivered it to my condo this morning when you were sleeping late again, as usual. I met her by my car and we packed it all in a cooler. The other box has all I need to make my sangria. Now why don't you get a fire going over there, and I'll get this ready for us."

"Should we drag the table over by the fire?" she asked him, but he shook his head.

"Nah, I'd rather drag the fake fur quilt off of the bed and sit on that, right in front of the fire. That okay with you?"

She shook her head. "You think of everything, don't you? I thought I was the organizer, the party-planner par excellence. You make me look like a slacker!"

She went over to the fireplace and, using the wood next to it, had a cheery blaze going in no time. She looked at Alexander, who was busy slicing fruit for the sangria, while the microwave made enticing smells fill their cabin. "How did you know I know how to build a fire?"

He popped a maraschino cherry into his mouth and smiled at her. "You told me you were a Girl Scout, then Katie's Girl Scout leader for years, remember? I *do* listen when you talk, you know. It might not seem like it, because sometimes I have trouble concentrating when the blood leaves my big brain to rush down to my little brain, but I pay attention to you."

She walked over to touch him, and he drew her into his arms for a long kiss and fondle.

"I guess I'd better watch what I say from now on, then." she said, once she was able to free her lips. "I just assumed you were like most men, and saying 'uh-huh' in all of the right spots to make me think you were listening."

He let her go, and turned to pour sangria into two glasses, handing her one. "How do you think I got to be such a great salesman? You *have* to listen to what your clients tell you, or you'll miss opportunities to knock their socks off. Most of them expect you to fill the needs they tell you about, but it's the needs they don't even know they have, until you fill them, that get you the big commissions."

He checked the microwave. "It's ready. Let's eat!"

They sat by the fire and had a picnic of Patti's wonderful foods, drank Alexander's secret recipe sangria and thoroughly enjoyed stuffing themselves until neither of them could eat another thing. They pushed the dishes into the corner. Alexander stretched out, pulling a pillow off the nearby couch and lay back sighing with contentment.

"You made coffee, didn't you?" Tegan asked. When he nodded, she got them two mugs of it, and brought them over to sit next to Alexander and snuggle with him, pulling the fake fur covering over their legs. They spent some time quietly watching the flames dance in the fireplace.

"This feels more like a honeymoon than an anniversary," Alexander said. "Since I never had much of either one, I'm only guessing, mind you. But this is how I imagined it would be."

Tegan turned to look at his face. "You were married, weren't you? Didn't you have a honeymoon?"

Alexander continued to watch the flames, "No. We were too poor. We were married in the church during Mass on Saturday, then we had family over to my parents' house for dinner. We stayed in a Holiday Inn Saturday night, and by Sunday we were in a room in her parents' house, where we lived for two years until we could afford an apartment. I was back at work on Monday morning."

He sighed, taking Tegan's hand that was resting on his arm and kissing her knuckles.

"We didn't do much for anniversaries either, because there was always family around. Once we got into the apartment, she started pressuring me to get her pregnant before we even had any furniture in it."

"How old was she?"

"She was only eighteen when we got married. But Hispanic women have an earlier body clock than you white women. At first, she would try to press her case by getting me so horny I would forget to use a condom. I figured out pretty quickly what she was doing, and once I refused to play that game anymore, we started fighting."

"So that's why you got divorced? You didn't want kids?" Tegan asked, and felt an ache in the pit of her stomach, as she realized just how deeply his aversion to fatherhood ran. Dreams she hadn't even realized she was harboring, crashed and she felt slightly ill, and not from the food and drink.

"Yeah," he answered. "We were too young and poor, and I didn't want to end up like my father, surrounded by starving children and having to put them to bed hungry."

He looked at her face and was surprised at the look of concern on it.

"It turned out for the best, though, for both of us. Maria got married again pretty quickly after the divorce, and she has about a dozen kids. She's happy, and I'm happy. It was hard to live through, but what doesn't kill you, makes you stronger, right?"

Tegan, her face turned away from him, said softly, "Not always."

Alexander pushed himself up to sit next to Tegan, and he put his arm around her shoulders. He took a deep breath to steady his nerves before he spoke again.

"Tegan, your husband left you because he's gay, right?"

She pulled away quickly, and her eyes flashed with anger. "She told you? I'm going to kill her! That's none of your business!"

He felt a stab of guilt, and wondered how she had found out about his little chat with Katie.

"I told Patti I didn't need you to find out about that! If I wanted you to know, it was *my* secret to tell, not hers."

He shook his head, and tried to turn her face up to him, but she turned away. "Tegan, listen to me, Patti didn't tell me anything."

"*Right!* And you just guessed on your own, huh? How stupid do you think I am?"

"You're the most intelligent and most beautiful woman I have ever met. That's how I figured it out. It was only a guess, but your reaction just told me I had guessed right."

He was more determined this time, as he turned her face and made her look at him; he looked deeply into her eyes. "Hear me out. Tegan, you are the kind of woman men have wet dreams about. You are the one we imagine while we are masturbating... a woman who enjoys sex even more than we do, who knows how to take her pleasure and gives back a hundred-fold. And you never ask for anything in return. Most men spend their whole lives looking for a woman like you, and most never find her. Your ex-husband had you to himself, and had children with you. He should have been happy to die in your arms, from his final orgasm in extreme old age. But he left you. 'Why?' I asked myself. And his being gay was the only reason that made sense."

"Maybe I just wasn't woman enough for him," she said defensively.

He realized that in some deep, dark part of her soul, she still believed that.

He smiled as he shook his head. "That's not possible. You are almost too much woman for even *me* to handle, but I'm going to continue to give it my best shot and hope that even though I'm older than you, I can keep up with you."

She was quiet, and still looked unconvinced.

"Honey, I had never had a multiple orgasm before I met you. It's happened to me at least a couple of times now. The first time I thought I must be having a heart attack and I was getting ready to meet my maker!"

She smiled, but her eyes still looked troubled.

"I had read it was possible for men to have them, too, but I figured the guy who wrote that was just lying, to try to one-up every other man, making us think *he* was getting something we weren't. But now that I've felt it, I crave more. I crave *you*. I told you, you're like an obsession with me, and I can't get enough of you. So there's absolutely no way a heterosexual man would have left you. End of story."

She shook her head. "But how could he have made love to me so convincingly, if he didn't want me? We met in college and got married right after we graduated. We were married for fifteen years. Why did he lie to me, and say he loved me? Why didn't he ever tell me, when he knew he was gay?"

"Maybe he didn't know he was."

"How could he *not* know? If what I have read is right, and you are born that way, how could he not know? I thought men couldn't fake orgasms."

He smiled at her. "We can't. At least not the way women can. But I'll bet he figured as long as he made love to you, that made him *not* gay. Part of the whole trouble with our society is that it is considered a choice, or a crime, or morally disgusting, to be gay. People just are, or they aren't. There's no place for judgment of any kind. But if there wasn't such a prejudice against it, men especially wouldn't try so hard to deny, even to themselves, what they feel."

She still looked unconvinced, but she was listening.

"Tegan, I'm speaking as a Hispanic man and we invented the whole concept of machismo. But I'm telling you the truth, as I see it now."

A look of total shock and disbelief was on her face, as she gasped, "Oh, my God! Not you, too?"

He laughed heartily at the look on her face and finally gasped, "No, my sweet. Not me. I just told you I crave your body, your smell, your taste. Everything about you gets me hot, including just sitting around talking to you."

She looked relieved, but still troubled.

"Let me explain. My youngest brother, Roberto, took me aside at a family party a few years ago, and I can still remember how full of self-hatred he looked when he told me he had been with a man and liked it. Now keep in mind that Roberto, like many Hispanic men, had started having sex with girls when he was in high school. But he was twenty-three years old, and having a total identity crisis. He told me he was afraid to tell anyone else in the family, and he was contemplating suicide, because he was so shocked by his own desires."

Tegan looked at him in disbelief. "He had been with women for all of those years, and had only just figured it out it wasn't what he wanted?"

Alexander nodded. "Yes. I'm embarrassed to admit I didn't take what he was telling me at all well. I was disgusted by the whole idea, and shocked that someone I knew so well, in fact had shared a bed with for years, along with our two other brothers, was attracted to men. I said all of the textbook things you should *not* say. I asked him if he was sure. I asked him if he wanted me to buy him a prostitute, to remind him how being with a woman felt. I asked him if he thought it was a phase he would grow out of, if we just let him experiment a little. Even though we were raised Catholic, I asked him if he wanted me to try to find one of those centers that evangelicals believe in, where they are supposed to be able to teach a man how *not* to be gay anymore. In short, I totally disappointed my youngest brother, who had always looked up to me, since I was the oldest. He made me promise not to tell anyone else, and he left the party right after that."

Alexander stopped to take a long drink from his sangria, since it seemed to be a better choice than coffee, considering the topic.

"What happened? He didn't kill himself, did he?" Tegan asked.

"No. But I went online when I got home, and stayed up all night, researching websites that dealt with gay issues. Of course, the gay pornography pop-up ads were gross, but I had to know what my brother was going through. He had trusted me, and I felt like I had let him down. I was afraid if I didn't know what to say to him the next time, he might do something stupid and final, and I wasn't about to let that happen to someone I loved so much."

He sighed. "Then I called him and asked him to come to my place for dinner, telling him I wanted to talk to him. He tried to back out, but I was insistent... okay, I told him I'd come and find him and drag his skinny ass over there myself, if he didn't come voluntarily. And

140

we spent the whole night talking. Finally, when it was getting light out and we realized we had been up all night, I offered to let him sleep for a few hours at my place. When he offered to sleep on the couch, I insisted he sleep in my bed with me, since we had done that for years, and he had never done any groping that I was aware of. He's my brother, for crying out loud! Just like I'd never grope my own sister, he'd never be attracted to his own brother. Homosexuals are not necessarily depraved, though some are, just as some heterosexuals are. And not all homosexuals are pederasts, just like not all pederasts are homosexuals. Those are actual sicknesses, whereas being gay is something that's programmed into the DNA, like hair or eye color."

He paused, to get up and throw a few more logs onto the fire and to get the pitcher of sangria for refills. He sat down next to her, and poured sangria into both of their glasses.

"And after that, I went with him when he told the rest of our family. Some took it well, some took it badly. But I made it clear, as the eldest, that anyone who thought he should *not* be a part of our family anymore was out of line, and they were the ones who should leave. I told them Roberto is our blood and always will be, and that hadn't changed. Gradually, most have come around. Our brother, Jorge, still doesn't talk to Roberto much when he's in town and the family gets together, but considering seven out of eight siblings have not rejected him, Roberto considers himself pretty lucky."

He stopped and watched as Tegan studied the flames in the fire. "So you see, I'm pretty sure your ex was denying what he was, even to himself, for years. He probably figured marrying you and having kids with you, would make him forget all about his urges. But instead, what you try to deny most about yourself usually comes up to bite you in the ass later. His biggest mistake, in my opinion, was hurting you so much. He should have been honest with you, and told you once he realized he was gay; certainly, once he started to act on his desires."

Tegan sighed heavily, and kept looking at the fire. "He started having an affair with Bill while we were still married. He had stopped initiating sex soon after our second was born, just when my sex drive reasserted itself and I was going nuts. Then he stopped even responding, so that's why I have so much lingerie back home. I tried everything to get him to want me, and nothing worked. We had been living like a brother and sister for over three years when he told me he had met someone he wanted to be with more than me, and he was leaving me. At first he didn't say anything about being gay, but I kept begging him to give me another chance to be the kind of woman he wanted. I offered to change everything about myself, if he would just tell me how."

She stopped and took a deep, shaky breath. "He broke down and cried, and told me he was gay, and it was a man he had been having an affair with, and there had been other men before him too. He had been living a lie with me, and couldn't do it anymore. And then he walked out of our house and left me alone."

Alexander cursed the man who had done this to her, softly in Spanish for a time while he held her and stroked her hair. She felt tears start to trickle down her face, but she wiped them away.

"I told him I was done crying over him after the divorce. I don't talk to him any more than I have to. If we didn't have kids together, I wouldn't ever want to see him again."

Alexander gently tilted her face up again, so he could look into her eyes. She looked away. "No, Tegan, look at me, please."

She finally looked at him, and he leaned down and kissed the tears out of her eyes. His lips gently brushed hers, as he whispered words of love in his first language, something he had not done for years, but for feelings that came from so deep in his soul, it seemed more natural. Gradually, he felt the tension leave her, as her body once again became pliant against his, and he felt her beginning to respond to his words… to his touch… to his love.

142

By the light of the warm, crackling fire, they made luxurious, smooth, satisfying love on the fur cover, and when they joined their bodies into one, this time it was a joining of souls as well. When he shuddered and groaned in harmony with the roller coaster ride of orgasms that Tegan was dragging him on with her, Alexander realized his suspicions were correct, and he had finally met the one woman he wanted to spend the rest of his life loving. Now he just had to figure out how to convince her, so they could begin to create their happy-ever-after.

Thirty-four

The one good thing about the fact that neither of them had ever been cross-country skiing, was they were both just as bad at it. They rented the skis, poles and boots right after breakfast on Saturday. By lunchtime, they were both bruised and sore from falling so many times. Tegan had just missed running smack into a tree by sitting down quickly, and while painful, did not break any of her bones. They turned in their equipment, then went back to their room to soak in the whirlpool tub. They ate a light lunch of the leftovers from last night's Patti-food, then gave each other massages on their sore body parts, which led to more highly satisfying lovemaking.

They went for a hike in the woods to enjoy the sylvan quiet of the snow-covered forest, and found a bench to sit on so they could watch the sun slowly set over the snowy horizon. They didn't talk much all day, but they did laugh a lot while skiing and both enjoyed the feeling of peaceful acceptance they radiated at each other while they walked and sat in the cold winter air.

They had dinner in the rustic lodge restaurant, and afterwards built a fire in their cabin telling each other their deepest fantasies, to either act them out, or keep them in mind for the next time. Alexander was immensely grateful Tegan didn't understand Spanish very well, since he found himself telling her that he loved her, and he wanted to spend the rest of his life with her. Her only response was to moan, scream and call out his name while they drove each other to ever higher levels of pleasure.

Since they overslept on Sunday, they checked out then drove into the nearest town to find some breakfast. They found the local university's radio station on the way back home and spent part of their long drive back listening to, and arguing over, the merits of the various new music today's kids were listening to. Once that station faded, Alexander put an early Led Zeppelin CD into his car radio, and they both sang along with it.

Since Tegan had no car for him to return her to, Alexander insisted on driving her home. He pointed out to her since it was getting late that was their best chance of beating her kids home. He had no desire to spoil the memories they had created over the week with an unpleasant scene involving her ex-husband and their children. Tegan agreed with him, telling him she wanted to be home before everyone else, to give herself time to change back to Mom, after being Tegan, the sex symbol, for a week.

It was dark by the time they pulled into her driveway. Alexander helped her carry all of her things into the house, then with the lights still out, he pulled her close for a final goodbye kiss and grope. With great reluctance, he forced himself to leave and didn't look back as he headed back into the city, to his condo which had never seemed emptier and less inviting.

Tegan watched out the window as he headed back to his lap of luxury life that didn't have any children in it. She sighed with unhappiness that he could want her so much, but not want her children. They were a package deal, that much she was sure of. Any man who wanted to have only her had to either wait ten years until Kevin was away at college, or had to be content to have only a small part of her life... one weekend a month was all she could spare.

145

The next four weeks were going to drag on forever, since she already missed Alexander's presence and his touch. Tegan sighed again and turned on the lights in order to get her things unpacked and put away before the children got home.

Thirty-six

Katie strode into the house, covered in attitude. She had talked John into taking her to a hair salon in the city and she had gotten a punk haircut and pink highlights dyed into her blonde hair. When Tegan had not immediately raved about how wonderful it looked, Katie had flown off the handle at her, insisting since Bill thought it looked very cool, Tegan was just jealous, or too old to appreciate real style. She had also gotten her cartilage pierced in her left ear at a piercing booth that operated out of the same beauty salon. Tegan had allowed her to get her ears pierced once, for her twelfth birthday, but they had argued over cartilage piercing, since it was more prone to infection. Tegan had advised her to wait a year to see if she still wanted it.

Tegan raised her eyebrows at John to let him know this wasn't over, but they would be discussing this turn of events in the very near future. John had sidled towards the door, and once Katie made a very big deal out of kissing and hugging him, and telling him what a *great* time she had with him and Bill, he left to drive back to the city. Kevin had immediately disappeared into his room upstairs, and the only sound was from his computer being fired up to play his new games.

This left Tegan and Katie alone in the living room, getting all of Katie's gifts from John and Bill in order so she could carry them upstairs. Katie made Tegan look at all of the tee shirts she had received, and Tegan winced at the slogans, like "Come and get me," or "Super-bitch," that were on the shirts. She was even more shocked at the tiny shorts that had words on the butt, like "Fresh and tasty," and the more demure, "Look here!" She tried to explain to Katie that her middle school principal might take issue with some of the clothes, were she to wear them to school. Katie took that as a challenge and started yelling at Tegan.

"Honestly, Mom. I'm *not* a child anymore! I'm going to be a teenager before you know it. Stop treating me like a baby. I can wear whatever the hell I want!"

They were both shocked at what had just come out of Katie's mouth, and Tegan had to fight the urge to slap her daughter for casually swearing in front of her. She herself had been slapped for cursing many times during her adolescent angst-filled outbursts, and she had sworn if she ever had a daughter, she wouldn't be as strict as her parents had been with her.

Katie spoke up first, trying to explain, saying, "That's the way Bill talks all of time. He's around teenagers all day, since he's the manager of the game store where he works. He says they all talk like that and it's cool. They're only words, Mom. Don't you get it?"

"Fine," Tegan said tightly, "But there's a time and a place for words like that, and it's never in front of your mother... not until you're eighteen and ready to move out of the house. Until then, since I watch my language around you, please do me the same courtesy. I know those words, too, but they are like spices in food... to be used sparingly, for emphasis and flavor. They are *not* to be used casually, in everyday conversation with adults. And *please* don't ever talk like that in front of your grandparents!"

"Jeez, Mom, you are so old-fashioned. Bill says Dad used to be like that, too, but now that he has a younger roommate, he has learned how to loosen up. You are just too uptight. You need to learn to relax. Chill, Mom, just chill."

Tegan bit her tongue many times during that rant and quietly helped to carry Katie's things upstairs to her room. Then Katie shut the door in her face, and immediately the sound of loud rap music came blasting through her door.

Tegan called Patti and they commiserated, each drinking a glass of wine in their respective kitchens, as they both cooked dinner for their ungrateful children. Tegan promised to call Patti with details of her week away when the kids were back in school in the morning. She thanked her for the food that had been so welcome in the cabin.

Patti giggled, "Don't mention it! He *did* pay me for it, you know. Just business. And may I say again, he is one hot Latino, girl! Let me know if you ever get tired of him. I hear they don't mind women with a bit of extra cushion for the pushin'. This is one time I'd be *glad* to take care of your leftovers."

Tegan was surprised she felt more than a twinge of jealousy at the idea of anyone else being with Alexander. She tamped those feelings down, telling herself that unless he was willing to wait ten years until she was free to be with him, she had better prepare herself to lose him sooner or later. The thought depressed her so much, in addition to Kevin's indifference, Katie's attitude and John's lack of parental guidance that she continued to drink wine with dinner and finished off the bottle while she soaked in the tub afterwards.

Thirty-seven

Since John's week with the kids had not ended until the fourth of January, there wasn't a visitation weekend in January at all. Alexander had not thought of that, and was not pleased to discover he had to wait until early February to see Tegan again. This meant they would be seeing each other too early to celebrate Valentine's Day together. Nevertheless, he was desperate to see Tegan, so once he had spoken with her during the day in early January, he made some plans for their February weekend together.

Tegan was preoccupied when he picked her up at the commuter station and this did not bode well for his plans. After they loaded her bag into his car and she fed the parking machine, he got on the highway to drive into the city. They drove in silence for a while. Finally, he had to know what was going on.

"What's got you so deep in thought? Something bothering you?" he asked, putting his hand gently on her knee to try to get her to focus on him.

She sighed heavily. "What's *not* bothering me these days? That would be a much shorter list. Katie got a new haircut, dyed her hair pink and got her cartilage pierced in one ear, while she was with John. She did it all because Bill told her it was cool; he also told her I'm too old-fashioned, and her dad used to be like that until he moved in with him. That asshole! How dare he criticize me to my own daughter? I'm really tempted to tell her what's going on between the two of them, but I'm not sure how much she knows about what being gay means. Besides, that might make her not want to see her dad anymore, and I can't hurt him like that... he loves her and Kevin too much."

Alexander continued to rub her leg while he was driving and tried to ignore the erection that was trying to rob his brain of what little blood it still had in it.

She continued. "When I asked John what he was thinking when he let her do all of that, he told me to lighten up and said I needed to get a life so she could live hers. What the hell? She's only twelve! Time enough for her to live her own life when she's eighteen and moves out of my house, so I don't have to see what she's doing!"

She turned to look out the window on her side, "And then there's Kevin. I swear, I think since I only have a sister, I'm not really good at figuring boys out. All he ever wants to do is play those damn computer and video games, and he never talks to me at all. Katie talks too much, trying to pry into my life, like she knows I'm seeing someone, and Kevin ignores me, like I'm just an ATM, cook and maid."

Suddenly, Alexander pulled the car off the highway, made a quick turn and parked in the nearest parking spot in the lot he pulled into. He turned to Tegan and, in answer to the questioning look in her eyes, smiled and tilted her face up to kiss her long and hard, while his hands roamed under her clothes. After a few very sweaty moments, he put the car back into gear and headed back onto the highway.

Tegan was leaning back in the seat, smiling, when she asked him, "What was *that* all about?"

He glanced over at her and smiled, "You needed to be reminded that being a mom is only a part, though admittedly a large part, of who you are. You are also the woman of my dreams. And since I only get to see you for two days out of the month, I want to be sure that Tegan, the sex-kitten, comes to my condo with me."

She looked offended. "Sorry if I'm bothering you with my troubles. I guess since you only want to see me for one thing, I'd better get myself naked and give it up ASAP, right?"

He shook his head and sighed in exasperation. "No, that's *not* what I mean. But I think we need to continue this discussion when I'm not driving, so I can concentrate on what you are saying, and really listen to you. Not when I'm fighting late Friday afternoon rush hour traffic into the city."

"Fine!" She said peevishly. "That way you can start touching me, and I'll just forget all about my little problems and think only about pleasing you."

That was the last thing she said while they drove into the city. Alexander kept glancing over at her, but she kept looking out of her window. He wisely refrained from saying anything else that might get her more upset.

When they got into his neighborhood, Alexander told Tegan he had pre-ordered some dinner for them, and he stopped in front of a tiny Italian restaurant that had a line of people waiting outside. He double-parked his car and told her "Wait here, I'll be right out." He pushed his way past all of the waiting customers and shook hands warmly with the mean-looking bouncer at the door. He went right in and returned a few minutes later, carrying two bags of food that emitted glorious smells once they were in his back seat. He climbed into the car and drove the rest of the way to his condo.

Since he had to carry the food upstairs, and Tegan had her overnight bag, they both had their hands full in the elevator on the way up.

"That's probably a good thing," Alexander thought to himself, studying Tegan's profile, while she studiously avoided looking at him.

"She doesn't look much in the mood to be getting groped right about now."

Once in the condo, Alexander went in the kitchen to put the bags of food on the counter, while Tegan took off her coat, then followed him.

"Should I get naked now, or do you want to eat first?" she asked, as if the answer didn't matter to her at all.

He looked at her sharply, then shrugged. "Is this how you plan to be all weekend? I suppose as long as we do get to have sex eventually, I can hold my own with you for some extended fighting. But I think you are taking out your general bitchiness on me, when it's not me that you are upset with."

He turned to get two glasses for the wine and expertly opened the bottle he had taken off of the wine rack.

"What makes you think I'm not upset with you?" Tegan asked angrily.

He looked at her again, then poured the wine into the two glasses and handed one to her. "What did I do?"

She stalked out into the living room area and Alexander shrugged again, then followed her, to sit on the couch that faced the chair she had perched herself on. She nervously tapped one foot, while she struggled with what she was going to say.

"It's more a matter of you being just *one more* person I have to please. Everyone wants a little part of me and I'm running out of parts. Sometimes I feel like there's no parts left for me." She shook her head. "I'm not explaining this well at all, am I?"

He took a sip of his wine, to give him a minute to think of how to respond.

"What if I told you I want more than just a little part of you?"

She looked at him intently. "What do you mean? How much more?"

"As much as you are willing to give me. Or to share with me."

"I can't do that, you know that. I have to think of my kids first."

He noted dryly. "They don't seem to be giving much thought to being grateful to you these days, do they?"

"That's not the point. They are heading into their teen years, and I always knew this was going to be the bumpy part of the trip. I remember being a teenager. It was damn hard to figure out who I was, and who I wanted to be. I was a real rebel for a long time... my older sister was the perfect one who always got good grades and never gave my parents any trouble. I don't think she even had sex until she got married... maybe not until she got to college, anyway."

He smiled at her. "Somehow, I don't think you waited that long."

She shook her head, a tiny smile on her lips now, "No. I got tired of masturbating all the time and decided to see if having sex with a boy would last any longer and give me more relief from the constant yearnings I had. I was seventeen when I first went all the way with a boy, and after that, since I wasn't enjoying it half as much as when I 'did' myself, I spent the next few years trying to get better at what I was doing, so I would enjoy it more."

She took a few sips of her wine before she continued, "I don't think I even had an orgasm with a guy until I was in college. But once I did, I was like a kid in a candy store. It's so ridiculously easy for a woman to get laid, as opposed to a man, who has to work for it. All I ever had to do was walk into a bar and send off some signals that I was available. I swear, it must have been pheromones or something. Before long, they'd start appearing around me and I'd have my pick of who to go home with, or to take home with me."

Alexander shifted around on the couch, trying to ignore the throbbing erection in his increasingly tight pants. "I'd be even more jealous if I didn't know that everything you have done, every man you have ever had, has led you to my condo and my bed. Since I don't

154

intend to ever let you leave me, I guess I'll just chalk it all up to practice, so you would be able to blow my mind and make me realize you are the only woman for me."

She looked at him in shock. "What are you saying?"

He got off of the couch, and knelt in front of her chair. "Tegan, honey, I was planning on waiting until after dinner to talk to you about this. In fact, I was planning on waiting until we had enough sex, so I would be able to think clearly again. But I don't seem to ever be able to do things the way I plan to when you are around. You are the most exasperating woman I have ever met. You make me crazy, then you give me more pleasure than I have ever thought possible."

He paused to shift around, since his knees were hurting from the pressure of kneeling on them.

She waited, expectantly.

"Tegan, I want to marry you, someday. But first, I want to get to know your kids. I want you to get to know my family. I want the whole world to know that you, Tegan O'Neill, are officially off the market, since you belong to me now. This is February, the month of Valentine's Day. It's the right time for me to tell you that I love you, and I don't want to live without you anymore."

He leaned forward and, smiling at the shocked expression on her face, he kissed her. Predictably, once their lips met, the heat flared between them and before long they were rolling around on the floor, tearing off each other's clothing and working towards their mutual goal of joining their bodies together again. Alexander barely remembered to put on the condom, then he spread her legs and pushed his way into her, past any resistance her body might give him.

Tegan began screaming from the moment he was flush against her body. He looked into her face then, at her eyes squeezed shut, at her expression of ecstasy, and he told her, "See, *mi querida*. You *know*

I'm the only man for you. No one else can make you scream the way I can. Make me come with you, my hot woman! Make me lose control... make me lose myself in you!"

And she did. Repeatedly.

Eventually, they stopped to reheat the food he had picked up and ate it, accompanied by the wine they had both forgotten about. After that, they moved into the Jacuzzi for their traditional after-dinner soak.

Much later, when they were lying exhausted and panting on the waterbed, Alexander rolled to his side, and used one hand to gently stroke Tegan's face, murmuring words of love to her, in Spanish.

"*Mi querida... mi cariña... yo no puedo vivir sin usted... te quero...*"

Tegan opened her eyes, and there was sadness in them as she looked into his. "You don't mean that. You are just using the final tool in your arsenal to be the winner in this game, right?"

He raised his eyebrows. "Game? What game?"

She looked intently into his eyes. "You are the alpha, remember? I can't ever forget it... just being with you, I'm overwhelmed by your masculinity. I'm putty in your hands and I have to force myself to remember it's just a game with you."

He began to feel the first stirrings of anger. "What game? You mean to tell me you think I'm just saying what I think you want to hear?"

"Yes. You told me you always win by finding out what the other person wants, then giving it to them before they even know it's what they want. You know my kids are important to me, so you tell me you want to get to know them. But you forget; I know why you got divorced. You shouldn't have told me, if you wanted me to believe you."

He sat up. "Tegan, I was in my early twenties. I was dirt poor. Look around you; I'm not poor anymore. And that was half my lifetime ago... I'm in my forties now. Things are totally different." She sighed heavily. "I'm too tired to keep on arguing now. Let's get some sleep, then we can talk again in the morning."

"Come and sit by the fire with me and talk to me now, Tegan. This is too important to *not* finish."

She shook her head and yawned, "No. If I go out by the fire with you, we'll just start up again and no talking will happen. I'm too tired to think anymore. Just let me get some sleep, okay?"

She turned her head away from him and closed her eyes.

He looked at her for a moment, in stunned silence, then he got up from the bed and left the room.

Tegan started to cry the moment he left. The tears started as a trickle, then she sobbed as if her heart was breaking, because it was. She had fallen in love with a man who had no desire for children; and now, because the sex was good, he wanted to move into her life and make her children deal with him. They were giving her enough trouble the way it was, and he wanted to add the additional complication of knowing their mother had a new lover.

John would be happy, of course, since it would help him feel less guilty about what he had done to her. But Katie would be upset and Kevin might even turn from his computer games long enough to tell her she had no right to a life of her own. What had started out as such an innocent thing, a sexual fling, an affair, had now grown into a monster that was strangling her with its strength. She hadn't meant to allow her feelings to get involved, and now he was playing with her, telling her what she wanted to hear to prove he could do it.

Then what? Would he spend some time hanging around once he had to start interacting with her kids? Or would he start finding excuses to stop coming around the instant they started to make demands on him, the way they did on her, on John, even on Bill. He was not the kind of man to let them walk all over him, the way they did on John and Bill. So if they got difficult to deal with, she could easily see him deciding it was too much trouble and going back to the twenty-somethings in the bars he had been playing with before she became his latest prey.

Eventually, she fell asleep, after she had shed all the tears she had in her body and she felt strangely empty. But she knew what she had to do in the morning.

Thirty-eight

Alexander got a shot glass and his bottle of aged tequila down from the cabinet, and went to sit on the futon in front of the fire. Feeling this angry, with no way to deal with it, was unusual and unsettling for him. He had told her how he felt, damn it! He had bared his soul and she had rejected him!

Rationally, he knew why she had. She was still not over the pain of being rejected by her ex-husband, but he had no plans to ever leave her. She had to realize that. Couldn't she tell by the way they moved together, by the way their bodies were in total harmony, each cell resonating to the sounds coming from their counterparts in the other's body? They were perfect together. They belonged together. He had faced the truth of it, even though it had scared him, too. Why was she refusing to face the inevitable?

True, he had not wanted children years ago. But lately, he had been wondering what he might be missing. He might finally be ready to take tentative steps towards becoming a father. He wouldn't know for sure until he tried, but she wasn't even going to give him a chance to try. What an unreasonable, exasperating woman!

He needed to teach her a lesson. Maybe he wouldn't call her in March… let her wonder why. It would be torture in the extreme for him, when already, less than an hour after making love with her, he wanted her again. The knowledge she was in the next room, asleep in his bed, was an agony to him. He had to drink a lot more to avoid going in and waking her up to make passionate love. He continued to pour shots and drink them.

He cursed his situation, cursed her ex-husband, cursed her children, cursed her refusal to believe him and cursed himself for being such a fool as to fall in love with a woman who had trouble written all over her when he first met her. He had always gotten into trouble when he allowed his dick to do the thinking for him. He usually managed to keep it under his control, but those few times it overruled him were disastrous. This was the biggest disaster since his ill-fated marriage. Maybe she was doing him a favor by rejecting him. Maybe he should just walk away from her, try to forget about her. Let her go back to her annoying children and her unfulfilling life, and he'd go back to his glorious... what? Bachelor existence? Empty condo? Empty bed? Empty life? He sighed heavily and poured himself another shot.

Thirty-nine

Tegan was surprised when she woke up to find Alexander nowhere in sight. Then she remembered why, and what she had decided to do. She got up, padded quietly around the apartment and found all of her clothes. Alexander was asleep face down on the futon, snoring loudly. There was a mostly-empty bottle of tequila next to him, along with an empty shot glass.

She got dressed quickly and wrote a quick note to him; she placed the note under his shot glass, then took a long look at him lying there, naked. The lines of his body called to her in some primal place deep within her. She knew he was the only man for her. Their bodies belonged together. She had never felt so alive, so *whole*, as when he was deep within her, filling the emptiness inside of her with himself. Her need for him was a visceral, living thing and she was going to have to carry that inside of her for the rest of her life. So much for being the always-in-control woman she had imagined herself to be!

Her birthday was next month. She was going to be forty. She was going to spend the rest of her life regretting that she had let him go. But as much as he wanted her, he didn't want her children, so she had no choice in this matter.

Resolutely, she tore her eyes off his perfection and turned to walk out of the door, and out of his life.

She paused at the door, saying softly, "Goodbye, lap of luxury. Goodbye, dreams of a perfect union. Goodbye, Alexander Reyes. I will always love you."

Then she closed the door behind her and left.

Alexander woke up hours later, with a dry, furry feeling in his mouth, a nauseated stomach and a king-sized hangover that made him feel like his head was exploding after having been beaten with a mallet all night long. Lying down hurt, but when he sat up, he had to hold his head in his hands because that hurt even more. While he was taking deep, cleansing breaths, trying not to throw up and not to cry out from the agony in his head, he saw a piece of white paper under his shot glass. The sick feeling in his stomach was joined by a feeling of dread that squeezed at his heart and made his entire body go cold with fear.

With trembling hands, he reached for the note and read it:

> *"Dear Alex, I'm sorry for everything I put you through. You don't have to worry about how to get rid of me and my troubles. I'm taking them with me. You've won the game, but I can't play anymore. I will always love you, but my kids have to come first. If you still care, call me in ten years, when Kevin goes away to college. Until then, Tegan."*

Then he ran to the bathroom, and threw up.

162

Thirty-nine

For the next month, Tegan felt like she was sleep walking through her life. She went through the motions of being alive, but felt like she had died inside. She took no pleasure in anything, nor did she feel other emotions of any kind. She worked with Patti on their business and was as efficient as she ever had been. She dealt with her children as if she was a robot... doling out food, cleaning up their messes and hardly reacting at all when Kevin ignored her, or Katie acted up, trying to get a rise out of her.

When John came to pick up the kids for their weekend with him, even he noticed something was wrong with her.

"What's wrong, Tegan?" he asked when she let him in the door as they waited for the kids to finish fighting and drag the last of their stuff down the stairs.

She looked at him with empty, emotionless eyes. "Nothing."

"There's something going on. Katie has been telling me how worried she is about you for months. Now you are acting like a zombie. She worried you are going to crack up or hurt yourself, from the strain of not ever letting yourself relax. Is that what has happened? Should I talk with Patti and schedule an intervention for you?"

She stared at him as if she was looking through him. "Why should you care?"

"Because you are the mother of my children," he said loudly. "What affects you, affects them. And despite everything that has happened between us, Tegan, you are still one of my closest friends. You may not want to be, but there is more history between us than even I want to acknowledge. You know me better than almost anyone else, and I know you that well too. There's something seriously wrong with you, when you don't even want to fight with me, or be bitchy."

She regarded him dispassionately, then looked away. "I'm fine. Nothing to worry about. I'm just tired, that's all."

At that moment, the room was suddenly filled with hormones and noise. Their kids raced into the room and hugged their dad; then both talking at once, they grabbed their various bags and headed out to the car. Tegan followed them and waved at them as they pulled out of the driveway. She turned and slowly walked into her house, locked the door and went to lie down in her bed, fully-clothed, where she lay until the house was dark. Then she got up slowly, changed into her pajamas and lay back down on her bed, where she stayed until morning. She slept very little, but kept her eyes closed and tried very hard not to think about anything at all.

Forty

On what would have been the weekend for Tegan to spend with him, Alexander decided he needed to get out of his oppressively empty condo. He changed after work on Friday, then took himself out to dinner at his favorite neighborhood Italian restaurant; then he hit the bars. What struck him as he walked into one after another was the sameness of it all. Nothing had changed in the six months since he had stopped frequenting the places. The faces were still the same: bored, desperate and lonely people were everywhere. He was shocked to realize he had never noticed that before.

Instead of scouting out a beautiful woman, he sat at the bar and watched what was happening all around him. Women displayed themselves like peacocks, thrusting out cleavage here, a well-rounded derriere there. They all wore too much makeup, which looked harsh on the younger ones and scary on the older ones, who were trying much too hard to look younger. Around them circled the men, with the alphas in the immediate areas close to the more attractive women, and the other men positioning themselves closer to women they hoped would be more accessible for them.

The level of desperation rose with every passing hour, and as he moved from bar to bar, the situation was always the same. Attractive women would notice him, then give him "the look" that was supposed to draw him closer, so they could decide if they were interested or not. Other alpha-males would draw themselves up, trying to appear more formidable, in order for him to realize he should *not* challenge them for the women. And always, he would ask himself, "Am I interested?" His most reliable compass stayed limp, despite all of the hormones in the air and the pulchritude all around him. And no matter how many drinks he had, he felt as sober as a judge.

At the last bar he hit, the closest one to his house, a young blonde woman he vaguely recognized from some time last year or the year before, he wasn't really sure, walked up to him and gave him a kiss. Surprised, he almost felt a glimmer of interest, then he looked into her face and saw emptiness, along with lust.

She smiled at him, a little drunkenly, and said, "Hey, you're Big Al, aren't you? I thought I recognized your sexy self when you walked in. Long time, no see. You're not alone tonight, are you?"

When he nodded, she moved in front of him again and he felt her hand grasp his reliable compass that stubbornly refused to react to her stroking in any way.

Gently, he removed her hand, and smiled at her sadly. "Sorry, honey. Not interested tonight."

Her eyebrows shot up into her hairline, "You were plenty interested the last time! I'd love another look at that penthouse of yours. I remember the view was really cool. What say we head out to your car and let's see if I can't get you more in the mood, huh?" With that, she crudely pantomimed oral sex.

Alexander had to fight himself not to laugh at her. As it was, he smiled. "Sorry. I told you, I'm on my way home now, alone. I'm tired."

She did not react kindly to being rejected; he guessed it might possibly have been an unusual occurrence for her. "Too tired? Maybe you're just too damn old! You are looking a lot grayer and more

166

wrinkled than the last time. What happened, did you burn that picture that used to be in your attic?"

Now he remembered her. Who else would have heard of "The Picture of Dorian Gray"? She was an actress in the local theatre scene. And yes, being rejected was not something she was used to at all. In fact, he had ardently pursued her one night and beaten off half the bar in order to be the one to take her home with him. She had been lively in bed, but drank way too much and passed out on him. In the morning, she had mumbled about having to get to her day job and left early. He had not been sad to see her leave.

He turned to the bartender and bought her another drink. He gave it to her, saying, "Good luck, honey. I'm out of here."

He quickly walked out of the crowded bar, past all of the women who gave him a quick, interested look, and the men who glared at him and breathed a sigh of relief when he got back to his car and drove himself home to his empty bed.

In the morning, he swallowed what was left of his pride and called Patti to ask for her advice.

Forty-one

Patti had been sitting at her desk in her home office, pondering how on earth she was going to get Tegan, who was almost catatonic these days, out to a bar to celebrate her fortieth birthday on Wednesday, in four days time. Tegan had said just yesterday, when Patti stopped by to check on her while the kids were at school, that she didn't want any kind of birthday party. She was too tired, she said. How would they get a sitter for a Wednesday when Rosa usually didn't do weeknights? And whose house would the kids sleep at? Better to just let the whole thing pass unnoticed. No gifts, no party. Just another year older and more tired.

Patti was determined to do all she could to pull Tegan out of this funk, but she was beginning to be afraid it might take professional intervention. They had helped each other through the pain of their divorces, but this thing with Alex seemed to have pulled Tegan's heart right out of her. She was beyond pain. She was beyond feeling anything at all. She was just going through the motions of being alive, and that was seriously scary.

When the phone rang, she jumped, then she picked it up. "Hello? Parties by Pat-Teg. How can I help you?"

"Hello, Patti," said the familiar low voice. "How is she?"

"Alexander Reyes, you asshole! What the fuck did you do to her?" Patti was working on a serious rage against this man who had done so much damage to her best friend.

There was a heavy sigh, then he answered. "I asked her to consider marrying me. I told her I wanted to get to know her kids. I told her I love her and I don't want to live without her anymore." He paused. "I know, I know, I'm a beast."

There was a shocked silence. "You did?"

"Yes. Didn't she tell you?"

"*No!* She told me you both decided the affair had to end, because it was too hard to build a relationship with only one weekend a month. And that's all she will tell me."

She paused, considering how much to tell him, then realized professional intervention might not be needed, if she could manage to get them back together. After all Tegan had told her for the past six months, it was so blindingly obvious they belonged together, she was ashamed she hadn't realized it before... hadn't thought to call *him*.

Patti took a deep breath and decided to take action.

"She's acting like she's not even alive. She's like some kind of zombie for love. She looks like herself, but it's like there's no one home. I'm seriously worried about her. Even during the divorce, she was never like this. She was angry, she drank a lot, she ranted and raved, and cursed and cried a lot. But she never completely turned herself off, like she was dead inside."

Alexander felt alarm, then a glimmer of hope.

"Then, I guess I don't need to ask you if she's seeing anyone else, huh?"

"You idiot! Didn't you just hear me? She's missing you so much that she never feels anything anymore. It's like she's in so much pain, she decided to save herself by shutting down her emotions completely. I can't even get her to smile. And the day that I, Patti

Johnson, can't get a smile out of my best friend, with a well-told dirty joke or nasty reference to, say, the much-wondered-about body parts of our sexy young mailman, is the day I call in professional help for an intervention. Even John is worried about her. And Katie is frantic! Kevin has retreated into his own world. Believe me when I tell you, you need to do something to clean up this mess you made out of my best friend's life, or I'm gonna have to do you some serious damage!"

There was a long pause.

"What do you suggest I do? She's determined not to believe anything I say. She thinks I'm just telling her what she wants to hear, in some bizarre way just trying to prove that I can do it. She thinks I'll leave her right after I get her kids to like me, or right after they begin to annoy me."

"She told me you got divorced because your wife wanted kids, and you didn't."

Alexander exploded with annoyance. "That was almost twenty years ago, for Christ's sake! We were dirt-poor. I had grown up that way, and wanted to make sure I wouldn't have to live like that anymore. It wasn't so much that I didn't *want* kids, as I didn't want them *then!*"

"But you never had any after that, did you?" Patti, playing devil's advocate, asked to test him.

"I never met anyone else I even thought about wanting to have a child with. Until now."

"You don't plan to love her and leave her then?"

"In case you hadn't noticed," Alexander responded dryly. "That's what she did to me."

"And you're in pain, too?"

There was another heavy sigh. "Patti, last night I went out to the bars I used to hang around in every week, trolling for women. I tried to be interested, but none of them mattered to me. My dick stayed

170

limp, even when it got groped, and I went home early, alone, to my empty bed. I can't stop thinking about her. My job performance is down the toilet. I'm afraid to go visit Edgar, even though having family around me would be soothing, because I'm afraid I'll crawl across her lawn and beg her to take me back. And you know what? She'll think *that's* some kind of trick on my part, too! I honestly don't know what to do to get her to believe me. But I can't go on living like this either. That's why I called you."

Patti thought for a moment. "Well, I'm sitting here trying to plan a birthday party for her, for next Wednesday, when she turns forty. She told me not to plan anything, that I should just let it pass unnoticed."

"And are you?"

"Like hell I am! You only turn forty once! And if I don't throw *her* a party, she won't throw one for me either later this year, when I turn forty."

For the first time in weeks, Alexander managed a small smile.

"So, what are you going to do on Wednesday?"

Patti thought again, then made her decision and briskly continued. "I'm going to drag her even-more-bony-since-she's-not-eating-anymore-ass out to a bar, and you are going to meet us there. I won't tell anyone else you are coming, but you need to be there. I'll call you when I have set up the time and place, then you plan on getting there a couple of hours after we do. That should give me time to get some food and alcohol into her, so she will at least be a bit more life-like. Then it will be up to you. I don't care how you do it, but you have to save her. I think you're the only one who can."

Alexander smiled again, "I hope you are right. Now, along with being worried about myself, I'm worried about her, too. I have no idea how I'm going to convince her of it, but she and I belong together. We were made for each other. And I won't rest until she believes me."

It was Patti's turn to sigh. "That's so romantic! I don't suppose you have any brothers, do you? I mean besides happily-married Edgar?"

Alexander actually managed a small chuckle, "Yes, but Roberto is gay and Jorge is a stick-in-the-mud, whom I wouldn't dream of foisting off on a live-wire, firecracker of a woman like you. You'd eat him alive out of boredom. But believe me, Patti, once I get Tegan to marry me, I will turn my full attention to finding you a man who's worthy of you!"

Patti giggled. "Just don't plan on moving her out of the subdivision, okay? All of our friends are here and our business depends on us living close to each other. I don't care if you sell that house, since you might not want to live with her in the house her husband screwed her in, even though that was years and years ago. Buy a bigger house, but stay in the neighborhood, okay?"

"Presuming I can get her to an altar, I'd live with her in a mud shack, if it would make her happy. Since I know you make her happy, I think we have a deal."

"Okay," Patti continued briskly. "Let me make some calls, and get a place set up. I'll get some of the neighborhood women to go with us, and we can all car-pool. That way she won't be driving. Then you can insist on driving her home, or whatever. I'll also have her kids stay overnight with mine. Since it's a school night, they can go together in the morning. That way, if she happens to *not* make it home for the night, they won't have to find out. I'll just tell them all she was too drunk to be seen by young, impressionable children. Katie won't believe me for an instant, but tough shit. This is her mother's life we are trying to save here. No one has time to put up with her adolescent angst while Tegan is catatonic. We have to get Tegan back to normal. Then we can go on from there."

"Okay, Patti. I'm really glad I called you."

"I'm glad you called, too. I'm ashamed to say I didn't think of it first. But I believed her, and figured you had dumped her."

"That's what I was afraid she might have told you. That's why I didn't call you weeks ago. But this has gone on way too long. It's time to get things settled."

"So, I'll call you when I have the place and time. Let me worry about getting her there. Then you can worry about taking her out of there. And you had better be right about this. If she rejects you, and blames *me* for inviting you, I am going to take you apart, bit by bit, and scatter you on her lawn, so she can wipe her feet on you everyday."

"Sounds reasonable," Alexander responded dryly, "since I can't possibly be in any more pain than I am already. And remind me not to *ever* get on your bad side!"

Patti smiled. "Goodbye, Alex. I'll call you soon."

Alexander managed a tight smile. "Bye, Patti. I'll work on thinking up how to get my reluctant and stubborn sweetheart to believe my intentions are true."

Forty-two

"This had better work!" Patti said to herself, as she called up the restaurant she and the neighborhood women liked to go to on their ladies' nights out. She made arrangements for an area of tables to be set aside for them starting at seven on Wednesday night. She called around to their group of friends and invited everyone to come help her jolly Tegan out of the doldrums caused by turning forty.

"No need to embarrass her by letting everyone in on the reason for her state of mind," Patti thought, "Since most of us are not happy about the big four-oh."

Then she called Tegan.

"Hello," Tegan said, in a flat tone, when she answered the phone.

Patti took a deep breath, and launched into her pitch. "Hey, girl, get your shit together and find some clean clothes to wear. Or at least clean underwear. I've got us all booked in The Party House for seven on Wednesday for your big birthday celebration. You don't need to eat first, not that you've been eating anything lately... Katie snitches on you, you know. But we will feed you, and make you drink mass quantities of alcohol and you will enjoy yourself and thank all of your friends for making you feel special! That's an order!"

There was silence. "Patti, I don't think I feel up for a party, I told you that. Can't we just let it slide?"

"*No! Hell no!*" Patti shouted into the phone in her enthusiasm. "If I don't make a big fuss over you, you might forget to make a big fuss over me later this year when I face middle-age! And since there's no way in hell I would let you get away with that, you have to face the music and go out with us. There's no way around it, Tegan."

"But what about the kids? It's a school night, and Rosa's dad won't let her sit after ten on a school night." Tegan was grasping at straws, but at least her voice sounded a bit more animated.

Patti quickly shot down any arguments.

"I've already spoken to Rosa and it's fine," she lied. "Your kids can stay at my house, so I can get them all to school on time on Thursday morning. That way, if you are unable to get away from worshipping at the altar of the white porcelain gods, the kids don't have to find out about it. At least until they turn forty themselves, and go through the same aging crisis."

"I don't know, Patti," Tegan continued. "I'm still feeling really tired. I think I might be coming down with something…"

"Bullshit! This is just what you need to get you out of your bad mood. You need to get out, get some fresh air and do some partying. I'll make sure you drink enough alcohol to kill any bad bugs or viruses that you might be harboring. Tell the kids you all need to be at my house by six-thirty on Wednesday night, and I'll call you later to talk about what we are going to wear."

"Why?" asked Tegan.

"I'm thinking we need some kind of theme, like everyone wearing black arm bands or something like that. Let me think about it, talk to the other gals and I'll let you know what we decide, okay?"

"Don't I get any say in the matter?" Tegan asked petulantly.

"*No!* And no arguments from you either, old woman, or I'll knock your cane out from under you. I'll call you again soon. Looking forward to it! Par-tay! Par-tay!"

"Okay," Tegan said. Then she hesitantly added, "Patti?"

"What?"

"Thanks for being such a true friend."

"Aw, girl, don't start now. I'm gonna cry. I'd rather be doing that while I'm hugging you with one arm and hoisting my drink in the other. Bye!"

"Bye." And for the first time in weeks, Tegan actually smiled.

Forty-three

"Hello?" Alexander said, surprised his cell phone would ring on a Sunday afternoon and not at all pleased it had done so while he was at Edgar's house drinking beer and watching a soccer game in the family room downstairs. Edgar had just left the room when Juanita called him upstairs for a phone call. Otherwise, Alexander might not have even bothered to answer his phone.

"Alex, you need to help me! You're the only one who can!"

Alexander raised his eyebrows at the tone of desperation in Patti's voice.

"Does this help involve Tegan?" he asked.

"DUH!" Patti shouted into the phone. "What do *you* think? What else have I been thinking about, and working on for the past twenty-four hours? Of course it involves her, you big dope!"

Alexander cleared his throat. "And how may this big dope be of service to you, oh great and wonderful woman who cooks like a dream but has the social skills of a bull in a china shop?"

Patti giggled. "Oh, stop! It's just that all of my plans are going to fall through, if you can't talk to that pig-headed brother of yours and get him to let Rosa sit for all of our kids on Wednesday night. He's claiming she's got too much homework and he wants her in bed by eleven at the latest on school nights. Juanita usually goes out with us, so he knows we are usually out past midnight and he figures we'll be out even later, since we are celebrating such a land-mark birthday. He's refusing to let Rosa sit. What are we going to do? You're my only hope! Even Juanita's threats to make him sleep on the couch are useless."

Alexander smiled, becoming aware he could hear arguing going on upstairs.

"Well, as luck would have it, I'm at their house right now, sitting in the basement, waiting for Edgar to get back downstairs. It sounds like they are still discussing it right now," he said. "Let me talk to him. Once he gets back down here to watch the game, he'll need another beer, then he'll want to rant and rave about uppity women. I'll agree with everything he says and then I'll work on him."

"Thanks! I really need to know if you can get him to change his mind."

"Oh, I think I can. But I have to go. I hear doors slamming, so she's probably pissed and headed upstairs. Bye."

Alexander quickly closed his phone and was in the process of sitting down with a couple of cold beers when Edgar stomped down the stairs mumbling to himself. Alexander tossed his brother a beer, and Edgar plopped himself down onto the couch he had been sitting on, and began to complain.

"What the hell is up with women, anyway?" he said, by way of introducing a favorite subject of theirs. "They get so damn demanding sometimes! Aren't I the head of the house? Shouldn't I get to decide a few things around here?"

"Um, hm, "Alexander said encouragingly.

"Then, when they don't get their way, their first weapon is always threatening to with-hold sex. Shit! It's not like *they* don't enjoy it as much as we do. *We* aren't the ones to have multiple orgasms. They are! So what's up with that?"

Alexander felt his lips twitch, and he had to bite back his desire to brag to his brother. Instead, he asked, "What's wrong now?"

"Ah, 'Nita got a phone call from one of the neighbors... you know, Patti, the one who does such great cooking? She's throwing a fortieth birthday party for Tegan, the other gal from their party-planning company, on Wednesday night, in a bar. She wants Rosa to come over to her house and stay with all four of their kids until she gets home. But I know those hens. Once they get in a group and start drinking, they'll be out to all hours of the night partying. And Rosa is only fourteen. She needs to be in bed by eleven on school nights. That's one of the few rules I'm allowed to enforce around here, and so that's one I'm strict about."

Edgar looked at his brother beseechingly. "Is that really so unreasonable?"

"Well," Alexander tried to think fast. "I'm not sure I'm the one to be asking about that, not having any kids and all. But I'm going to have to agree with Patti and Juanita on this one, and ask you to reconsider; maybe let Rosa spend the night there, so she can sleep there, too. That way, she could get to bed by a reasonable hour and the ladies can have their party."

"*What?*" Edgar regarded his brother as if he had just been betrayed. "Why? Why should you care?"

Alexander took a deep breath, then continued. "Because it would be a great, personal favor for me if you let her do the baby-sitting that night."

Edgar just stared at him.

Alexander smiled ruefully. "Okay, I'm going to explain. Remember when I had that party for a potential client, and Patti and Tegan did the work for me?"

Edgar nodded. "Yeah. Last year. I was the one who told you to call them."

Alexander nodded, too. "Yes. And I'm going to be forever in your debt for doing that. You see, I've been seeing Tegan ever since then, on the weekends her husband has the kids."

Edgar's jaw dropped.

Alexander laughed at him. "I know, I know. You're wondering why I never told you."

Edgar nodded, then opened his beer and took a drink.

"Remember when you wanted to know what was up with me when I was here for Thanksgiving? Why I drank too much and pissed off our *madrecita*?"

Edgar nodded again, drinking more of his beer.

"That's why. I saw her walking down the street with her ex, and I didn't know who he was, but I was so jealous that another man was with her, I lost control of my temper. I started drinking to try to keep myself from running after them and beating the shit out of any man who might be trying to take her away from me."

Edgar finally found his voice, "And this has been going on for, what, six months or so?"

Alexander nodded. "We had a fight last month. Tegan thinks I'm just toying with her. That I'm not serious about how I feel about her. We started out just having an affair, but that was *her* choice, not mine. She was afraid to let her kids find out she was dating anyone. She didn't want them to get hurt again. I went along with it, until I realized it's *not* just a game for me with her. I'm going to the party on Wednesday night, a little bit after the gals do. Hopefully, Tegan will have relaxed enough by then to give me a chance to explain myself to her."

Alexander stopped to take a drink of his beer, too, and smiled when he glanced at the TV and realized the game had been over for a while and neither of them had noticed. "If everything goes the way I want it to, she's going to be your next sister-in-law. So I'd consider it a huge, personal favor, if you'd bend your rules, just this once, and let Rosa sit for the kids on Wednesday."

Edgar whistled softly. "Does anyone else know about this?"

Alexander shook his head. "Only Patti."

Edgar got a wicked smile on his face, "So I know prime gossip *before* 'Nita, for once? And I can tell her I'm not only *not* sleeping on the couch, but I'm not gonna tell her what I know, until she puts out? *¡Dios mío!* I've waited my whole married life for an opportunity like this!"

Alexander laughed. "But you two have, what, six kids?"

Edgar shook his head. "Seven."

"You have sex all the time! What's so special about this?"

Edgar regarded him pityingly. "You'll find out, once you've been married a while. Longer than five years, I mean. Marriage is a game of love also, but a different kind of game than you're used to playing. Relationships with women *always* involve a game, but they are the ones who make up all of the rules. They hold us by our dicks and we follow along with them. If we are *very* lucky, every once in a while we get dealt a trump card, and brother, you have just handed me a huge one! I'm going to milk it for all it's worth! 'Nita is going to have to give me some serious head before she gets one word out of me on this one."

Alexander had to laugh at the expression of pure joy on his brother's face. "So, does this mean Rosa can sit?"

"Hell, yeah! In fact, I'm gonna go up there right now and tell 'Nita I've reconsidered. Then I'm gonna tell her I know some *major* gossip, but she's not going to get a word of it out of me, because she was threatening to make me sleep on the couch. Maybe I'll tell her *she* has to sleep on the couch. Let's see how *she* likes it!"

With that, Edgar bounded up out of his chair and started running up the stairs, two at a time, yelling back over his shoulder, "Thanks, bro! No debt! We're even!"

Alexander shook his head and smiled. The thought of playing a whole new game with Tegan was too much for him and he felt himself getting hard just thinking about it. He scrolled down to the last number that was listed on his phone and called Patti to tell her the good news, and to find out where and when he would have the opportunity to change his life.

Forty-four

Tegan took a long time figuring out what to wear to her party. She usually dressed for comfort, but somehow being comfortable didn't seem important when she was going to be the guest of honor and people were bound to have cameras and phones with cameras with them, to catch her in embarrassing actions. She finally decided she would wear something a little bit sexy, to show her defiance at turning forty. Not that she wanted to attract any men tonight, but at least if any of them looked at her, she would know forty didn't mean dead, just well-aged, like fine wine.

What she decided on was her favorite pair of jeans that hugged her butt, but had enough room in the legs for her to comfortably sit on a bar stool without feeling like her thighs were ten feet wide. She wore a black thong under them, but told herself that was just so she wouldn't have any panty lines. Then she chose a black halter top she didn't have to wear a bra with, but the black color concealed the fact her nipples were going to be poking through it the minute she got into the sure-to-be-chilly pub. She dug through her closet to the back where she kept her supply of stuff from when she was married and trying to attract a man's attention, and found her black lacy jacket that provided just enough warmth to keep her happy until she drank enough to feel warm for the rest of the night. She chose her shoes for the comfort, thinking there was nothing worse than drinking at a party and having to worry about losing your balance on high heels.

She looked at herself in the full-length mirror in her room and suddenly remembered the last time she had studied herself in it, when she had been putting her outfit together for her strip dance, that had led to...

"*No!*" she told herself. "I'm *not* going to think about him tonight. It's over. If it wasn't, he'd have at least called, to try to talk me into something. I haven't heard a word from him, so obviously we are through."

She sighed heavily, as the weight of unhappiness that sucked all of the life out of her settled itself into her stomach like a lump of lead. She did some deep breathing exercises she had learned in yoga classes, and tried to force herself to think about other things. She remembered her best friend in the whole world was worried about her, and had planned this party to try to cheer her up. She owed Patti big-time for all she had been doing lately... taking the kids back and forth and letting them stay at her house for tonight. Patti had been giving her the time and space she needed to pull herself back together, and even though she still felt like her life was empty and depressing, she resolved to try to enjoy herself, at least for Patti's sake.

Then she resolutely straightened up her shoulders and walked out of her room to hustle the kids out the door, so they would be at Patti's house by six-thirty.

Forty-five

Alexander took a deep breath to steady his nerves as he walked into The Party House that night. He wondered what it was that made all bars and pubs smell the same. Was it a combination of spilled beer, stale cigarette smoke and desperation?

"No," he told himself. "Not desperation. I'm not going to think any negative thoughts tonight. I've always been the alpha-male, the one who can walk out of any place with any woman I want. Tonight will be the same, only the woman I want tonight is going to try to fight me. So much the better. I love a good challenge. And if Edgar is right, it's time for me to stop playing this game and learn the rules for a new one. I'm going to use everything I've ever learned about the rules to this game and then I'm going to break every one of them if I have to. But Tegan O'Neill, you are coming home with me tonight and every other night for the rest of your life."

He looked around the room and the first woman he recognized was his sister-in-law. She saw him at the same time and she waved. He strode purposefully over to her table.

"*Hola Alejandro*, you gorgeous hunk of man. Long time, no see!" She gave him a big hug, then a wicked smile played on her lips.

She leaned towards him and spoke quietly to him, which was not really necessary, since the music from the juke box was so loud.

"Thanks a lot for letting Edgar in on your little secret, and not me! He's been torturing me with it ever since."

He smiled at the expression on her face, "You don't appear to be suffering too much from it, though."

She sighed happily. "In the eternal struggle between men and women, I say *'Viva la Différence'*!"

He nodded towards the other tables. "Where's the guest of honor?"

She shrugged. "Who knows? I haven't seen her for a while. But Patti made sure she ate something, then we bought her a few drinks. She's got to be around here somewhere."

He looked around, studying the women all around him who were drinking, dancing, and in general having an excellent time. Finally he spotted Patti at the other end of the room, close to the bar, when she started to wave frantically at him and gestured for him to move over to where she was.

"What took you so long?" she demanded when he got close enough to hear her. "I just hope you're not too late!"

He gave her a puzzled look, "You told me to get here at nine. It's eight-forty-five now. What's up? Where's Tegan?"

Patti gestured in the direction of the bar, and said, "Over there, in the middle of that huge crowd of men. The sharks started circling the minute she got loose enough to start dancing. I keep trying to drag her out of there, but they've stopped letting me get close enough to talk to her. The last time I saw her, she was doing shots."

He glared at Patti. "She doesn't *do* shots. That's too high octane for her, she says."

She nodded at him. "I know that. You know that. But you can't tell her anything right now. She's out of control. And with *that* crowd, I'm worried about gang-rape. Or someone putting some drug in her drink. You've got to get her out of there."

He took a deep breath, then started to move purposefully towards the group of men who were cheering. As he got glimpses through the crowd, he realized they were cheering when Tegan did a shot... then they would line up another one and goad her on until she downed that one, too.

A low rumble started in Alexander's chest, and he realized he was growling, but no one could hear it in here over the noise. No matter. He was going to rescue his woman and no man on earth was going to be able to stop him tonight.

He pushed his way through the men standing close to Tegan and stopped short when he saw her. She was thin and pale and he remembered Patti telling him she hadn't been eating much. But her face had color from the alcohol, and she was breathing fast from the excitement of being the center of attention for so many horny men. He realized she must be riding on the high of their pheromones right now and he had to get them to leave her alone, because she wasn't going to leave with him voluntarily at this point.

He wasn't immune to the attraction she was exerting on the crowd, because his erection became insistent and painful when he saw the tiny black halter she was wearing that barely covered her pointy-hard nipples, both of which begged for a man's mouth. Her jeans hugged her hips and accentuated her curves in a way that made his mouth water. And the fact that every man there was hoping to sink himself into her that night, made Alexander's growl become louder and more audible.

A few of the men around him heard him, and wordlessly withdrew, recognizing the danger in staying where they were. He pushed his way closer to her, and some of the men said things like, "Hey, stop pushing!"

He gave them his most alpha-glare. "Beat it. She's mine!"

Some started to argue.

To them, he said, "That's my wife there. Get out of my way, or I'll have to hurt you."

In that way, he got most of the men on the periphery to give up the game and leave, looking for other women who wouldn't be claimed by an obviously angry, large Hispanic man.

That left about five men in a tight circle around Tegan and they were the ones paying for the shots, and lining them up in front of her.

All of a sudden, Tegan saw him and stopped smiling. She got a cold, brittle look on her face and she swallowed the closest shot with a defiant glare in his direction.

He moved closer to her and suddenly there was a big, blond man directly in front of him, who looked him in the eye and pushed at his shoulder with one finger.

"Who are you?"

He fixed a glare on the man in his way, and said. "Let me pass."

The man glared back at him. "No. We found her first."

"Hey, Alex, it's my birthday! These guys are helping me celebrate. They don't think I look like I'm forty. Do you, boys?" She gave them all a flirty look, and it was all Alexander could do not to start punching them all out, for the sheer lust they all radiated at her, before they turned in a unit to face him.

At that point, Patti pushed her way through the crowd and grabbed Tegan's arm, saying, "Hey, honey, why don't you come to the ladies' room with me?" She smiled and winked at the men. "You *know* we women always go to the ladies' room together." She pulled Tegan off her seat, and half-led, half-dragged her through the crowd towards the back of the bar and the sign for the restrooms.

Alexander heard Tegan protesting. "But I don't need to go!" But he had more important things to worry about.

The men now looked at him, sizing him up. He had never been so angry in his life; he knew he must look formidable, because some of them wavered in their scrutiny and looked away. But as always, there were a few who didn't know when to quit, and they began to talk about him loudly to each other.

"Ah, he doesn't look so tough. Look at that watch. And his gray hair. He's a just a rich old man."

"Yeah, but he looks Mexican."

"He smells Mexican, too. Money doesn't change the smell of a spic."

"I don't think we have anything to worry about from him, boys. Just that pushy broad that keeps trying to drag the birthday girl away from us before we get to give her our presents." There was some nasty laughter.

Alexander kept a tight lid on his temper, trying to remember that spending the night in jail was not a part of his plan. Through his teeth, he said, "That woman belongs to me. I'm going to take her home now. And none of you can stop me."

"I don't think so!" snarled the man who had pushed at him earlier.

"Yeah, you may be a spic, but there's only one of you, and you're old."

"You'd better take a hike now, wetback, or we gringos are going to have to show you a thing or two."

"How about I show you this?"

Suddenly there was an open switchblade knife in Alexander's hand and he had grabbed the big blond man and had him in a headlock, with the blade at his throat. The man stopped moving. The others just stared.

"Ah, he's not going to do anything with that," one of them said, sounding less than certain.

Alexander pushed slowly and deliberately, and the knife began to cut the skin of the man's neck. A couple of drops of blood appeared, trickling under the knife's blade.

"All right, all right!" said one of the other men. "We get the picture. You're taking her with you. Whatever. There's other pussy in here. Now let him go and we'll leave."

Alexander hesitated for a second, because his adrenaline was pumping so hard, he really wanted to hurt someone. It had been such a long time since he had been in a bar fight, and he was just angry enough to not want to stop. But at that moment, he saw Tegan leading Patti back over to her seat, and when she saw what was happening, she stopped in shock and her jaw fell open.

He let the man go so suddenly, he stumbled and fell against the man who had said they would leave. The blond rubbed at his throat, and they all grumbled as they quickly dispersed, leaving Alexander standing alone with his anger, his knife having gone back to where it had come from, just as quickly as it had appeared; he stood looking at Tegan and Patti.

Patti cleared her throat loudly, saying brightly, "Well, well, what a surprise! Imagine Alex knowing about this place, huh? You two must have lots to talk about. I think I'll get back to the other gals, and you can join us when you are ready." She quickly walked away, and Alexander and Tegan stood still, staring at each other.

Tegan was the first to talk. "What the hell are you doing here? It's my party. Who invited you?"

Alexander took a step towards her, and she stepped back. "I invited myself. I need to talk to you."

Tegan pushed by him, grabbed one of the shots still on the bar and drank it down. "Well, I don't want to talk to you!"

She grabbed for one of the other ones and Alexander grabbed both of them and threw them down his throat and swallowed, then fought hard not to choke from the heat. Oddly enough, the fire burning in his throat helped to put out the fire of his anger. What took its place was a lust so powerful, he wanted to lean her over the nearest bar stool and take her where she stood. He had fought for her, and he had won. It was so simple. She must realize that. She had to. His brain strained for enough blood to be able to explain things to her.

Instead, he did as the brain that held all of the blood in his body right now wanted him to. He grabbed her and pulled her close, and he kissed her, a brutal punishing of her lips, to make her pay for torturing him for so long

She fought him, at first, so he held her so tightly she wasn't able to move. Then, as she responded to him, as she had that first time, he let her arms go and they twined themselves around him, her hands on his shoulders, his back and his butt. He groaned, she moaned and they relearned the configuration of each other's bodies and began to move in anticipation of so much more.

With great difficulty, Alexander realized he had to get her out of there and to somewhere they could be alone, to talk... yeah, that's right... to talk. He grabbed her hand and started to lead her out of the bar. They walked past Patti, who waved at them both, and Juanita, who waved, then winked at him when Tegan wasn't looking at her. He led her out into the cold of the evening, and when she shivered because she only had on her halter having left her lacy jacket and her coat in the bar, he took off his sports jacket and wrapped her in it, while they waited for the valet to bring him his car.

Neither of them spoke the whole way back to his condo. He wasn't sure if she was too drunk to talk, or if she was brooding, but he didn't care. She was in his car, going back to his place and she was going to be in his bed soon, no matter what she might try to say about it. So he drove faster than was legal, and prayed for the state police with their radar to have either taken the night off, or decided to make a prolonged stop for donuts.

Finally they pulled into his parking spot and he jumped out to help her out of the car. The fact she didn't open the door herself signaled to him she was drunker than he had hoped she'd be. He opened her door and gave her his hand to help her out of the car. She stumbled into him, and in reflex, his arms went around her and they found themselves kissing and groping in the parking garage. Once they got onto the elevator, he groped her shamelessly, running his hands up and under her halter top, then down into her jeans. They were both panting once the elevator stopped.

He somehow got the door opened to his condo and they fell through the door. They were groping each other and starting to remove clothing, when suddenly she pulled back from him and got a terrified look on her face. He let her go, and she ran for the bathroom. He heard her puking up the shots she had been poisoning herself with and he busied himself pouring her a can of coke into a glass filled with ice to help settle her stomach. He heard his medicine door slam shut, so he assumed she was brushing her teeth, for which he was eternally grateful, since she wasn't getting off so easily tonight. He'd take her without kissing her if he had to, but he was going to have her tonight, even if she passed out. She belonged to him, and there was no way around that fact anymore.

A little while later, she opened the bathroom door, and stumbled out of it, to throw herself down backwards onto his water bed. He had been sitting on a chair in his room, waiting for her, sipping on her coke. He walked over to her, pulled her upright and handed her the glass.

"Drink up, my love. This will help settle your stomach."

"What is it?" she asked, while she took a few gulps, then belched loudly.

"Coke. That's all you can handle right now. Whatever possessed you to do shots? I thought you knew better."

She smiled at him ruefully. "Those guys were flattering me. They were telling me how sexy I am. I knew they were lying, but it was still nice to hear. You haven't even called me, so I figured even their lies were better than nothing."

"I haven't called you, because you said you didn't want to hear from me for ten years."

"That's not what I said. Or if it was, that's not what I meant. I wanted you to call me. I wanted you to come after me. I wanted you to tell me you couldn't live without me. I wanted you to miss me as much as I miss you. I can't eat anymore. I can't sleep anymore. Nothing matters anymore, because you don't want me anymore."

With that, she started to cry, at first a few tears, then with great sobs that wracked her thin body making him feel like the biggest jerk that ever lived. He watched her sob for a few minutes, then he did what he yearned to do anyway. He sat next to her on the waterbed, wrapped his arms around her and held her while her shoulders shook and her sobs threatened her ability to breathe. He held her until she stopped crying, and took great gasps of air to get enough oxygen into her lungs for her to breathe. He held her until she grew quiet and felt compliant in his arms. Until she began to wrap her arms around him also, and lean her head into his chest, and she bit at him through his shirt.

Then she used one hand to finish unbuttoning his shirt. "You fought over me tonight, didn't you? You had a knife. I didn't know you had a knife."

He groaned, since her hot breath and wet tongue were on his left nipple and his ability to think and to talk was rapidly approaching its limits.

"Yes. I'd have killed any man who tried to touch you tonight. You are mine. You belong to me now. No other man can touch you. No other man should even think about touching you. Oh, God, Tegan, don't you know how I feel about you?"

He pushed her over then and he began to strip her, running his hands under her halter top, then untying the ends from behind her neck and pulling it down in the front, to give him unfettered access to her breasts... her nipples jumped up in delight to see him again, and he had to reacquaint himself with the pleasures to be had from each one before he could move any further onto her body. He untied the bottom part of the halter top and threw it aside, then turned back to look at her, his eyes on fire from the passion that burned inside of him.

He moved to her jeans and with a little bit of cooperation from her in moving her butt up when needed, he removed them. Then his tongue licked a path from her knees up her thighs to her thong-covered hair. He pulled the thong off and dove into her with his tongue and was instantly gratified by her screams of pleasure as she raked her hands in his hair and called out his name. He was a wild man, making her come again and again, reasserting his dominion over the woman who now belonged to him, enjoying her every sound, relishing the control he had over her.

But it wasn't enough. Not nearly enough. With a mighty groan, he pulled back from her and stripped himself naked while she lay on his bed and writhed and moaned, bereft and craving his touch again. He crawled onto his bed, held himself over her and with one hand, turned her face to look at him directly in the eye.

"I love you, Tegan O'Neill. I fought for you tonight, and I won. You belong to me, and from this moment on, you always will. Tell me you realize that. That you accept what is, and what must be. Tell me how you feel about me."

"I love you, Alex. I'm yours, forever and ever. Now take me, please, before I die from emptiness."

And with that hard-won admission, he held her wrists down on the bed, pinioned next to her head and he sank himself into her heat, in one smooth movement. Immediately she began to scream, the clenching of her muscles driving him to the brink of insanity, as he fought his own senses and tried to keep control. Over and over he pulled back, then surged forward, feeling her meeting his every movement, feeling her squeeze him, then quiver with each orgasm, as she rode the roller coaster of pleasure up and down, and he felt her force him to join her in her waves of ecstasy. He felt himself reach the end of her, then he surged forward yet again. As had happened in the past, he felt the nub of her cervix turn towards him and begin to slurp at him greedily, wanting to draw every part of him into itself. And he wanted that, too. With a mighty roar, he pushed one final time into her, then he felt himself explode with pleasure, as his balls drew up tight to his body, and he felt the blast of heat shoot into her, to mark her forever as his woman. He shook and shuddered, and held onto her as she screamed and together they reached up to the heavens and touched the face of God.

Forty-six

It wasn't until the next morning, when Alexander woke up before Tegan, as was usually the case, he remembered he had not used a condom with her at all last night... not for *any* of the times. Her excuse could be her drunken state, but he had no excuse for himself. His first instinct was to curse himself for his carelessness; but then he had second thoughts about it, as he lay in bed with her head on his shoulder, her soft breaths blowing at the hair on his chest. He had to get her to marry him, he reasoned, and she would undoubtedly come up with some reason to refuse him. But if she was pregnant with his child, she would have no choice. He smiled.

What was it Edgar had said about every relationship between a man and a woman being a game? He had said the rules were different in this new game. Alexander had never been one to follow rules in any game. He preferred to make his own. But even in the game of love he had been playing for years, he knew an unplanned pregnancy was cheating of the worst kind, if it was done deliberately by one of the people involved... but he had *not* done it on purpose. She always made him lose control of himself; she had since that first time he had taken her, wordlessly and without permission. And he had not regretted it for an instant. She had shaken up his orderly, but empty, life and made him feel of things he hadn't thought himself to be capable. He had sworn to himself on the way into her party he would make her accept the inevitable, no matter how he had to do it.

Alexander glanced at the clock next to his bed and realized he should already be at work. He gently moved out from under Tegan's head; she stirred, but did not wake. He padded into his office and called his boss to say he would be in later today, probably not until late in the afternoon. Something had come up. He looked down at himself as he said that, and smiled at the unintentional double entendre. He was *always* up for her. Damn! No other woman had *ever* been able to match him, passion for passion... not even Maria.

He went into the kitchen, made himself some coffee and ate a quick bowl of cereal, before he called Patti to find out what time the kids got off school, so he would know when he had to have Tegan back in her house, recovered enough to be able to face them.

"So, are congratulations in order yet?" Patti demanded when he identified himself on the phone.

"No, she's still passed out," he answered truthfully. "But I told you, she's not getting away from me again. Whatever it takes is what I'm going to do. I hope you will be willing to watch her kids for at least one night this weekend, because I'm not sneaking around to see her behind their backs anymore. Today will be the last time I'm bringing her back home without them knowing about it. She's going to want to take a cab, but that's not open for discussion either."

"Ooooh," said Patti. "You are sounding so macho and possessive, you make *my* toes curl! And I'm not the one you want! She's such a lucky gal."

He smiled. "I hope she agrees with you, but I'm not sure she puked enough last night to *not* have a hangover today. She may not feel like a lucky gal when it hurts to open her eyes as much as it hurts to keep them closed."

"I know the feeling," Patti said ruefully. "When my alarm went off this morning, I wanted to throw it across the room. But I had to drag my aching self out of bed to get all four kids off to school on time. Lucky for me, Rosa had gotten herself up, because I probably was still drunk at five-thirty, when she woke up."

"How late did you all stay out, celebrating without the birthday girl last night?" Alexander asked. "And how did you explain it to everyone else?"

"Pretty late, and let's just leave it at that. And, well, let's just say between Juanita and me, we explained what was going on, to everyone's satisfaction." Patti giggled. "You, mister, have become the man of everyone's dreams now. The gorgeous hunk of man that delivers our mail is now number two on our fantasy top five, and everyone wants to know what *you* are like in the sack. Tegan is gonna have a whole lot of explaining to do once she gets back into the swing of things."

Alexander laughed aloud. "And they say men are perverts! Anyone who thinks that has never listened to a bunch of older women, I guess."

"Yep," Patti agreed. "Only you guys probably only talk about what you wish had happened. We give details that would embarrass the hell out of you, if you knew we were sharing them. But no worry. No one will try to get you away from Tegan. She's one of us, and we protect our own. Besides, if anyone got the idea to try, they'd have to go through me and Juanita first, and we'd soften them up enough so Tegan could finish them off herself."

"Well, as much as I'd love to keep chatting with you about the secret depravity that lurks behind suburban housewives' seemingly-innocent coffee klatches, I think I should go in and try to bring Tegan back to life. I'll have her back before three, so she should be there, hopefully lucid, before you drop the kids off."

"Okay, José," said Patti. "*Adíos.*"

He smiled at her impertinence. "Bye, and thanks for all your help."

He felt the sense of calm beginning to permeate his being again, as he sat and regarded his phone and thought about what he might say to the woman in the next room who was responsible for every good feeling he felt these days. He got up, got another can of coke ready for her and went into his room to wake her up.

"Tegan, honey? It's time to wake up," he said in a soft voice, knowing any loud noises would only increase her agony.

She moaned.

"Tegan, I have another glass of coke for you. Sit up and drink it, and it will help settle your stomach. Do you want something for your headache?"

"Yes," she answered him, as she pushed herself up to sit, took a quick sip of the coke, then fell back dramatically onto the pillow, covering her eyes with the back of her hand. "A quick decapitation should do the trick. Once my head is gone, I'll be able to think again, without this blinding pain behind my eyeballs."

He smiled, then he got up to get her some non-aspirin pain pills, since her stomach was undoubtedly still queasy. He returned, helped her to sit up again, gave her the pills and held the glass while she drank.

"What is the slogan on that one tee shirt?" he asked, amused. "Oh yeah, 'How can I be so thirsty this morning, when I drank so much last night?'"

"Sure, go ahead. Find humor in my pain," she said. "You'll be sorry when I'm blowing chunks all over your expensive carpeting."

Then she moaned again. "I *did* puke last night, didn't I?"

"Yes."

"But I made it to the bathroom?" she asked hopefully.

"Yes. Barely."

She sighed, took the glass of coke into her own hands and continued to drink it. "Good."

She looked at him, squinting at the bright sunlight that streamed in through the balcony doorway in his bedroom. "Then we made love, right?"

He smiled broadly at her. "Yes."

She shook her head. "Jeez! You took advantage of a drunken woman. You cad! I'll bet I enjoyed it too, didn't I? I sure wish I remembered it."

He raised his eyebrows at her and regarded her hopefully. "We could re-enact it right now, if you'd like. Maybe it would chase that nasty hangover right out of your body if we raised up your body temperature enough."

She shook her head, moaned at the pain that caused and put her head in her hands.

"I will not puke again. I will not puke again."

He shrugged. "Whatever you say, my darling. In any event, we'll have plenty of time in the future to re-enact last night's passion. In fact, I've already asked Patti to sit for you one night this weekend, so we can have a real date that I pick you up at your house for. Maybe I'll even bring you flowers, so your kids can see I really like their mother."

She started to shake her head again, but remembered herself just in time. "No way! Nothing has changed, Alex. Just because you rescued me last night from a fate worse than death, doesn't mean you can tell me what to do."

"Perhaps you have forgotten I fought for you last night, and won?" he asked dryly. "And you told me you love me, and you belong to me forever and ever? And that we made love all night to seal the bargain between us? That since you got me so wild and out of control with passion, we forgot to use any condoms?"

She had turned away from him to shield her eyes from the sunlight, but now she slowly turned back to him, her shocked expression letting him know she *did* remember.

"Oh, my God!" she said softly. "I forgot about that. You're right. What if I'm pregnant? What am I going to do now?"

He got up from the chair he was sitting on and sat next to her on the bed, using one hand to raise her face up to look at him, and resting the other on her shoulders. "Don't you mean what are *we* going to do?"

She took a long, shuddering breath. Her eyes filled with sudden tears.

"Tegan, I told you I want to marry you. I thought I meant sometime in the future, but the last month has taken a huge toll on me. My job has suffered and I can't eat or sleep either. I tried to go out and pick up other women, but none of them interested me, because none of them were *you*. You and I are not getting any younger and I don't think we need to waste any more time thinking about whether or not we are right for each other. I think we both know the answer to that. If you are pregnant, then we will get married before the baby is born. If you are not, we have more time to plan things. But either way, you and I are getting married."

He leaned over and kissed her lips, gently, since he figured even her lips probably hurt.

"Patti has made me promise we will live in the same subdivision, and that will be the best for your children, too. So we can begin to look for a bigger house right away. I don't want to live with you in the house your ex made you so unhappy in. I want our house to have only happy memories for you. I'll put my condo on the market while we look around, and hopefully, we can be in the new house and married before the end of the year."

He smiled at the shocked look on her face, then he kissed her again.

"Say something."

She slowly raised a hand to check her forehead with it, then to check his. "I'm not sure which one of us is more ill and delusional. You appear to be assuming we will get married, without even asking me if I want to. And you expect me to just roll over and accept your plans without question?"

"Tegan," he began, but she got up out of bed and started looking around for her clothes.

"No, I'm not going to listen to you anymore. I've got to get back home, so I'm there when my kids get home from school. The only thing I want from you is for you to call me a cab, so I can get back home."

"No, I'm going to drive you back home. Your kids won't get home until Patti drops them off at three. You'll be home and probably well on your way to being recovered by that time. There's no rush. Let me feed you something to help anchor your stomach."

"*No!*" She shouted at him. "You don't understand. I'm not going to sit around here and listen to you plan my life for me. I'm not one of your twenty-year-old bimbos. I'm a forty-year-old woman and I run my life, not you. I don't know what makes you think you can order me around. Maybe that's the way things are done in the macho culture you were raised in, but that's not how I was brought up. Now help me find my clothes so I can get out of here."

She stood there, pulling on her black thong, looking for her clothes, and it was all Alexander could do to *not* attack her, tear off the thong and make love to her again, to get her to stop fighting him. Instead, he strode over to her and grabbed her shoulders to make her stand still.

"Look at me, Tegan!"

She looked around the room, trying to locate her missing clothing.

He used his hand to raise her face, then he kissed her again, this time much less gently. When she tried to resist him, he imprisoned both of her arms behind her with one hand and tilted her face up again with the other hand.

"Honestly, Tegan O'Neill, you are the most annoying woman I have ever met! You know as well as I do, we belong together. You stormed into my life and changed everything for me, and now you pretend that you didn't notice. You didn't notice my life was empty until you were in it. You didn't notice I never wanted children before, and now I am hoping you are pregnant, so I can finally know what it feels like to be a father, now that I'm ready and have found the right woman. I don't want to sneak around like I'm ashamed of being with you anymore. I'm not! I love you, and I want the whole world to know, starting with your children. I won't ask to adopt them, because they love their father. But I will help you raise them, because I love you and they are a part of you."

He kissed her again, then again for good measure. She had stopped fighting him, but she still looked mutinous. "And I don't want to hear any more crap from you about some game you think I'm trying to play with you. You think I just want you to capitulate, so I can hug myself, knowing I won, then I'm going to leave you? Have some self-respect, woman! Don't you know how beautiful you are? How desirable you are? How much I want to be that man who dies happily in your arms, after my final orgasm, in extreme old age? My God, Tegan, what do I have to do, to say, to get you to believe me? Tell me, because I'm out of ideas. But don't tell I have to leave you alone, because that's just not possible anymore."

He crushed her to him, kissed her and felt her arms move around behind him. He moved backwards, sat down on the bed, then lay back with her on top of him. They continued to kiss and fondle each other until she stopped and looked him in the eye, with a very serious expression on her face. "Is this how you will always end our arguments? Making me touch you, so I lose control over myself?"

His lips twitched with amusement. "Well, it's worked up to now. Edgar told me being married long-term is just another kind of game of love between the sexes. He told me I'm going to have to learn a whole new set of rules and I'll have to learn them from you, because you women write the rules and make men play by them. But I've never been one to play by the rules. I make my own. If I can make you listen to me by touching you, then I'm going to do what works."

"And what if I pretend to listen to you, then I do what I want anyway?"

He smiled at her with an expression of anticipation. "Then I'll have to keep on making love to you frequently enough, so you don't have much time in-between, to disobey me."

"And what if I make you think I'm being obedient, then I disobey?"

He laughed and rolled over so she was under him. He held her arms up over her head and looked at her with love. "Then, Tegan my love, we will fight and have the extreme pleasure of making up over and over again. *¡Dios mío, mujer!* I didn't even know I was looking for a woman who would stand up to me and fight me as an equal. Now that I have had you, there's no turning back anymore."

He began to grind his hips into hers, then stopped at the sudden expression of pain in her face. "Still too hungover?"

She nodded, looking slightly nauseous.

Solicitously, he got up, offered her a hand and helped her up.

"Let's find your clothes. I'll take you out to breakfast, then drive you home, so you have plenty of time to shower, change and get yourself into your mom frame of mind."

She regarded him seriously. "Okay, Alex. But this isn't over yet, not by a long shot. When I'm not so ill, we are going to continue this discussion."

He smiled at her. "Anything you say, my love."

She raised her eyebrows at his seemingly meek compliance. Then they got dressed and went out for breakfast.

Forty-seven

Once she was home, Tegan took a quick shower to clear her head. She changed into clothes more appropriate for a mom. By the time the kids ran in the door, she was sitting in the kitchen, drinking another can of coke. Both kids got themselves food out of the fridge, then as usual, Kevin ran upstairs to get right back to his beloved computer games. Katie sat on a chair and pulled it up close to Tegan so she could look at her closely.

"Mom, you have a hangover, don't you?" she asked with disapproval in her voice.

"Yes," Tegan answered honestly. "But I'm feeling a lot better now."

"Patti looked like crap this morning, too. She got in really late last night. When did *you* get home?"

"I don't really remember, honey," Tegan began, then hoping to change the subject, she said, "Did you have fun with Rosa last night?"

"Yeah, but you didn't answer my question. And I'll bet you drank a whole lot last night. We learned all about getting too drunk to remember stuff in health class last semester. In fact, the teacher said girls, especially, need to be careful, since when they get that drunk, that's the time boys will try to take advantage of them, since they are too drunk to know any better."

Katie looked more closely at her mom. "So, Mom, did any guys get fresh with you last night? Or did you get too drunk to remember?"

Tegan started to get angry, as guilt made her blush. "That's none of your business, young lady! I'm an adult and what I do is my business."

Katie looked shocked, as her eyes widened. "Oh, my God, Mom! What's that big purple mark on your neck? Is that a hickey? We learned about them in sex ed class. And there's another one on the other side, too. How many guys were you with last night?"

Tegan felt ill again, as her blood started to pound in her head, and she tried to defend herself against the attack she hadn't seen coming. "I told you what happened last night is none of your business. Now, don't you have homework to get to?"

Katie jumped up, dramatically waving her arms around, as if to gesture to her friends, "See? This is what *my* mom is like. Her husband divorces her, for reasons unknown and she turns into this. How can I show my face at school? How can I look at any of the neighborhood ladies, when they know all about you? Am I the last one to realize that my mom is nothing but an alcoholic slut?"

Tegan reacted without thinking, and watched helplessly as her hand shot out and slapped Katie across the face.

"Remember that I'm your mother, Katie! Don't you *ever* say that to me again!" she shouted.

Katie looked at her, shock and anger fighting for control of her face. "Don't worry. I'm too ashamed of you. I'm *never* going to speak to you again.'

And with that, she ran up the stairs to her room and slammed the door loudly, locking it decisively.

Tegan sat numbly at her kitchen table until it got dark outside. Patti called and she let the machine take a message. She heated up some soup and called the kids to come down for dinner. Kevin came down, gobbled his soup without speaking, then ran back upstairs. Katie never came down. Tegan tried to eat, but found she felt even more nauseous than she had felt that morning.

While she knew, rationally, none of this was Alex's fault, nonetheless she had to blame someone, and she already hated herself enough. She was a failure as a mom, failure as a wife, failure as a woman, since she hadn't been able to keep her ex-husband interested in her. And if Alex hadn't rescued her last night, who knows how many men she would have been with? But he had come to find her, for his own agenda. He didn't want to let other men touch her, because he wanted her for himself. Now that Katie thought she was a slut, how could she introduce him to her children and hope to have Katie accept him, or their relationship? Her mental anguish only intensified her physical discomfort and Tegan went to bed right after she cleaned up the dinner dishes.

She lay in bed, not sleeping, and stared into the darkness. She felt too empty even for tears. Her life was a disaster; she felt herself sink into a bottomless pit of despair, and no one was there to throw her a lifeline.

Forty-eight

In the morning, Tegan got up when the alarm went off. She woke up her children and packed their lunches while they got ready for school. When they came downstairs, she had their breakfast cereals on the table. Kevin ate his quickly, told her "Bye, Mom," gave her a quick kiss, grabbed his lunch, then went outside to wait for Patti to pick him up. Katie pushed her cereal around in the bowl, then threw it out in the garbage. She grabbed the lunch waiting for her on the counter and defiantly threw that in the garbage, too. She picked up her backpack and walked out of the door to join her brother at the curb. Tegan sat in her kitchen, immobile. She showed no signs of life when Patti came into the house and poured herself a cup of coffee, sat down at her table and looked at her expectantly.

"Well, girl? What happened?"

Tegan looked at her friend. "I hit Katie yesterday." Then tears began running down her face.

Patti looked surprised and gave her a quick hug, "It's okay, partner. If I had a nickel for every time my parents hit me, I'd be rich. And I turned out okay. Most days I even talk to my parents! Of course it took years of expensive therapy," she smiled. Then she added, "She's a pre-teen. She's annoying as hell. So is Chelsea, who, I might add, I

209

have hit a couple of times myself. So it's not as big of a deal as you think."

Tegan shook her head slowly. "No, you don't understand. She was giving me the third degree about where I had been all night after my party. It was like she could tell I had been having sex. Then she saw these." She leaned her head in one direction, then the other and gestured at the purple splotches.

Patti whistled softly. "He gave you those? What an animal! Oooh, tell me all about it, so I can be shocked. What was he doing with his hands when he did that? And with his big dick?"

Tegan shook her head again. "No, you still don't get it. She accused me of being too drunk to know any better. She accused me of being with more than one man. Then she told me she's too embarrassed that I'm her mom, because," Tegan paused, taking a deep breath, "she said I'm nothing but an alcoholic slut."

Patti stopped smiling. She got up from her chair, hugged her best friend and held her tightly while the tears ran down her face. She stood there until Tegan stopped shaking, then she poured them both some more coffee and sat down.

"You are nothing of the sort. For God's sake, Tegan, you've done everything in your power to keep your kids from being exposed to what is a normal part of adult life. You have protected them from what made their dad leave you so they think he's the innocent one. You have forced a man who really loves you to sneak around like some kind of adulterer, because you didn't want your kids to be hurt if things didn't work out with him. You never gave him a chance to prove he can relate to them and you never gave them a chance to test him. Your only real mistake has been to love them too much, to put them before yourself."

She stopped, looking closely at her friend. "You *do* believe me, right? You have got to start putting yourself first, because right now

Alexander is the only one who is doing that and you have too much to lose by rejecting him. He loves you and he wants to marry you. And I think you should take him up on his offer, because he shows every potential of becoming the husband you have always deserved and the partner you really need to help you keep those kids of yours in line. John is useless, because he feels too guilty for breaking up their home. And he's too terrified they will find out the truth. He never lets himself relax enough to be a good dad to them. Instead of disciplining them, he gives them anything they want in order to make himself look good. This is a crappy situation for all of you. I want you to make the decision that is right for *you*, for a change."

She stopped to take a breath. "Alex asked me to sit for your kids this weekend. I'll watch them for you tomorrow night, so you can go on a real date, out in the open. But I think you should have him over for dinner soon, to give them all a chance to get to know each other. And if they ask you not to see him anymore, you tell them to mind their own damn business!"

Tegan managed a small smile. The phone rang, and she jumped up to answer it. Patti started to page through the newspaper that was on the kitchen table, until she heard the change in Tegan's voice. She looked up quickly.

Tegan was holding on to the edge of the counter with the hand that wasn't holding the phone. Her face was drained of all color. "Are you sure? No one knows where she is?"

She nodded. "Yes, I'll start checking places I think she may have gone. Thank you. I'll call you when we find her."

She put the phone down. "That was the middle school. Katie isn't in school anymore. She was in her first hour class, then she wasn't in her second or third hour classes. No one saw her leave, but she has disappeared.'

She looked beseechingly at Patti. "What are we going to do?"

Patti got up and pulled out her cell phone as she headed for the door. "I'm calling the mom brigade. We will comb the neighborhood. She can't have gone far. You stay here, in case she calls, or the school does. I'll check back with you as soon as I get everyone mobilized." Then she strode out of the front door.

Tegan sat back down on her chair and stared at the wall. Her life had just gone from being terrible to being a total disaster. She had almost been ready to believe Patti, that she needed to think about herself for a change. And now Katie was missing, and there wasn't anything more important in the world than finding her daughter, apologizing for hitting her and begging her to forgive her mother for not being perfect.

Within minutes, there were many women in her house, all with cell phones, mapping out areas of the neighborhood they were going to search. Juanita came over with Rosa, who told her she had been home with bad cramps, but she was willing to stay in the house and be the one to get the phone if it rang, so Tegan could join the moms out combing the streets looking for Katie.

They hit the streets quickly and methodically searched the yards, the garages, knocked on doors and asked if anyone had seen Katie. They searched the school grounds and the buses. They went into the stores that were close to the neighborhood, and asked if any of the storekeepers had seen Katie. The next hour was spent in fruitless searching for a girl who seemed to have disappeared off the face of the earth. No one came up with any leads. No one saw her anywhere. Tegan was in front of her house, getting updates from some of the other women and Patti was using the hood of her car for a table, drawing up maps of larger concentric circles, for the next round of searches. Someone had called the police, who had come over for a current picture of Katie, and they had said they would put her into the system, so an Amber-Alert would go out, with Katie's face being broadcast all over the networks, in hopes someone would call with a lead. But they wanted to give the moms a chance to find her locally first, since there was no indication of anyone abducting Katie... for now, she was just considered truant. She would not be considered a run-away until twenty-four hours had passed.

Suddenly, Rosa came running out of the house, holding the phone, yelling for Tegan. "It's Mr. O'Neill," she said breathlessly, as she grabbed her abdomen in pain and handed the phone to Tegan.

"John? She's was there? Where is she now?"

Patti and the other women held their breath, hoping for some good news.

"Oh, *no*! She didn't? Oh, John, where is she?" And Tegan began to cry, large tears rolled down her face as she nodded. "We've already gotten the police involved out here. You need to call them there, too."

She hung up the phone, and spoke directly to Patti. Everyone else heard, and for some it was a surprise; for others, it was a corroboration of what they had suspected.

With desperation in her voice, Tegan said, "John says Katie was there. He didn't know Bill had given her her own key to their apartment. Bill thought it would make her feel more grown-up. John got off work early today, so he went home and Bill didn't have to work today. They didn't even hear the door being opened, because they were in bed. Katie didn't say anything until she was in the doorway to the bedroom and she saw what they were doing. She started to scream at them, saying there wasn't anyone she could trust anymore. She told John she hated him, and would never speak to him ever again, then she ran out of their apartment. They barely took the time to pull on shorts and they chased after her, but she was gone. They have no idea where she might have headed off to. But she's in the city now, and hates both of her parents. Oh, Patti, what am I going to do? Where's my baby?"

Tegan fell apart, nearly collapsing in the driveway, leaning on the hood of Patti's car and sobbing. Patti was the first one to be able to move, as she grabbed her best friend and held her, telling her they would find her, they had to. Katie had to know her parents loved her. She was a sensible girl and would realize she had to come home.

Patti looked up in desperation, and asked, "Does anyone have any ideas how we can find Katie? *Anyone?*"

No one said anything for a few moments. Everyone was out of ideas. Then Rosa spoke up, slowly, as if she wasn't sure if anyone would listen to her.

"Call *Tío Alejandro*! He might know where to find her!"

Juanita hugged her daughter and grabbed the phone from Tegan's limp hand. "You're right. They're friends. They talk at our house all the time."

She punched in the number, then made a face. "It's his answering machine. He's probably at work. Rosa, where's the phone book?"

"Under the pile of magazines in the living room, where Dad left it the last time he had to call *Tío Roberto*."

Juanita tossed Tegan's phone back to Rosa and took off running towards the house. Tegan and Patti turned to look at Rosa, who was telling them, "Katie's been at our house a few times, helping me to sit for the younger ones, when *Tío Alejandro* has come over for dinner. He even told her to call him *Tío Alejandro*, since she told him she only has one aunt, and no uncles."

Tegan and Patti looked at each other and they both realized at the same moment just who was being called upon to help them look for Katie. Tegan opened her mouth to object, but Patti shook her head to silence her. "If he can, we need his help."

They waited for Juanita to return from making her phone call.

214

Fifty

Alexander was sitting in a meeting, part of the interviewing process for an important prospective client. His boss was there, as was the owner of the company, to show how much they valued the business that could be theirs if the man decided to accept their proposal and give them his account. Alexander was in the middle of presenting his part of the proposal when his secretary came into the board room, apologizing to all there, and handed him a note.

"She says it's urgent. I'm so sorry to interrupt!"

She quickly retreated out of the room.

Impatiently, he unfolded the note, and read what it said:

"Juanita says Katie has run away from home. She was last seen at her dad's apartment, but found him busy in bed. Any ideas where to look?"

With his mouth suddenly dry and his hands shaking, Alexander stood up. "I'm sorry. I have to go. Family emergency." He cleared his throat, "Uh, niece ran away from home. We're very close. Don't know when I'll be back."

He walked quickly out of the door and left the other men sitting in the boardroom. He didn't care. Nothing mattered anymore, except finding Katie and punishing her for torturing her mother. After he hugged both of them very tightly.

He ran down the hall to his office, yelling at his secretary that he was leaving. He grabbed his jacket and headed out of the office. He didn't wait for the elevator, but ran down the six flights of stairs. Once he got into his car, he dialed Tegan's home number. Rosa answered the phone.

"*Tío Alejandro!*" she smiled as she held the phone out to Tegan.

"Hello?" Tegan leaned against her car as she spoke. "Why there? Okay. We'll meet you there as soon as possible."

She looked at Patti. "He said to meet him at the Lincoln Park Zoo. He thinks she'll be in the lions' house. What the hell?"

Patti started to push Tegan into her car. "I'll drive. Juanita, can you pick up Kevin and my kids after school? Keep them until we get back?"

Juanita yelled, "Of course! Good luck!"

Patti was already pulling out of the driveway.

As they drove, Tegan dialed John's number on her cell phone. He picked it up on the first ring.

"Tegan! Have you found her?" he yelled into the phone.

"No," she answered dully, "but we are heading down to the Lincoln Park Zoo to look for her there, in case you want to meet us. We are just getting off the highway now."

"The zoo? Why there?" he asked, but she could hear him yelling for Bill to come back, that they needed to go look for Katie at the zoo.

"Rosa's uncle is a friend of Katie's. He was the one who suggested it. It might be a bust, but I don't know where else to look."

"Okay," he said. "We'll meet you there. Any special area, or just look everywhere?"

"What's her favorite animal?" she asked.

"Of course. The lions. Good thinking. See you there."

Tegan looked at the now-quiet phone. "Only it wasn't *my* good thinking." She took another shaky breath, tears falling unheeded down her face.

"I don't even know where to look to find my own daughter. What kind of mother am I?"

Patti patted her arm soothingly. "The kind who manages to find herself a man who is wild in bed, totally in love with you, proposing marriage and *still* he found the time to get to make friends with your daughter."

Patti smiled sideways at her. "Despite, I might add, your jumping through hoops trying *not* to let them meet each other. I'd think you did a pretty good job of things, girl. Once we find Katie, things will work out. You'll see."

Tegan only stared ahead of her and tried to remember to breathe.

Fifty-one

As he drove, Alexander realized he was thinking in two languages again. In times of extreme stress, he often reverted back to his first language, without realizing it. In one part of his brain, he was praying in Spanish for his hunch to be correct and for him to be able to find Katie, safe and sound, and return her to her mother. He was also praying for her mother *not* to have a nervous breakdown, since she had sounded very near to breaking on the phone. And with the conscious part of his brain, he was pondering in English.

"So *this* is what it feels like to be a father?" He felt gut-wrenching pain, as if a hand were squeezing his entire torso and even breathing was difficult. His heart was pounding, and his hands were shaking on the wheel, as he drove way too fast to get to the zoo. It was mid-day, so the traffic downtown was the usual... clogged, drivers all irritable and they crawled along from light to light. He was afraid to hit his horn, because if anyone had gotten out of their car to threaten him, he was afraid he would kill them just to use up some of his adrenaline before it poisoned him anymore.

He felt violent and dangerous, and very, very afraid. He knew that somehow, someway, *he* had to be the one to find Katie. She was mad at her father; she was mad at her mother. He was the one adult she trusted, that she was not yet mad at. When she found out about his relationship with her mother, that would surely change. But for now, he had to find her and convince her to go back home.

Finally, he pulled off the street and parked his car in the lot by the zoo. He ran from the car to the entrance and hurriedly dug his membership card out of his wallet, almost dropping everything on the ground in his haste. No matter, he'd have left the credit cards on the ground and gone back for them later, because nothing else mattered except finding Katie.

He ran towards the lions' house and prayed in both languages that she would be there. Since it was a nice, sunny day in early March, there were lots of moms with strollers and toddlers wandered around enjoying their new-found ability to walk independently. Many looked at him with interest as he ran by them, eyes wild, intent on only one thing. When he saw the lions' house, he finally slowed to a trot to allow himself to catch his breath so he would be able to talk to Katie, presuming he found her.

He pushed open the door, and walked into the silence of an almost-empty building. Most of the lions were outside, sunning themselves. Since there weren't many animals inside to look at, the visitors weren't in there either. A quick look around failed to find any sign of Katie, so he ran back outside and circled the building, not looking at the animals, but searching the areas all around the outside lions' areas. None of the benches had Katie on them. None of the rocks or patches of grass showed any sign of her. He didn't have a picture of her with him, so he couldn't ask anyone if they had seen her. He realized he looked like too much of a wild man for any of the moms to talk to him, when they began to pull their children protectively out of his way as he ran by, mumbling to himself.

"Katie, where are you? You want to be a lion. So where are you?"

Disappointed, but still determined, he pushed open the door again and went back into the almost-deserted building. This time, he searched in all of the corners, and paid special attention to the benches. At the opposite end of the building from the door, he saw a backpack under a bench. Holding his breath, he slowly walked closer, looking all around him intently and realized there was a flash of color on the other side of the guard rail that separated the visitors from one of the lions' cages. He drew closer and saw there was a tiny figure sitting huddled down, wedged into the corner nearest the wall and the railing. The figure wasn't moving, but just sitting there.

He drew closer, hardly daring to breathe. Once he got close enough to see the streaks of pink in her blonde hair, he knew it was indeed the missing girl. He let out a quick, silent breath of relief, along with a thank-you prayer. Then he moved over to lean on the railing.

"Just because you are on the other side of the railing doesn't mean you are one of the lions, you know," he said conversationally.

There was silence, as if she hadn't heard him. He tried again.

"I thought you wanted to *be* one of the lions, not be food for them. Being devoured and digested is *not* a good way to be like them."

He leaned over the railing to get a good look at her. "Don't you think it might be a good idea to come over to *this* side of the railing, before the lions get bored outside and notice you in their territory? You know, lions aren't the only ones who don't like strangers in their house, but they are pretty aggressive about it, or so I've heard."

He was just getting ready to reach over and pull her bodily out of harm's way, when there was a sudden, shaky intake of breath, as if she had been crying and didn't want him to know it.

She spoke in such a quiet voice, he had to strain to hear what she was saying.

"Sometimes it's not the strangers in your house that hurt you."

He nodded, then offered her his hand. "True. Why don't you take my hand and come over to sit with me on a bench, and you can tell me why you are here."

She looked up at him and he realized he wasn't going to be angry with her; he couldn't be. She looked like a terrified child who had seen the foundations of her life crumble and she was left wondering how she could possibly trust anyone anymore. Her face was drawn and pale; her eyes were dark with tears, both shed and unshed, and the anguish in her face made his heart swell with love and a fierce desire to protect her.

He waited quietly for a few moments, holding out his hand until his arm began to shake with the strain. She finally let out a long breath, then slowly rose and put her hand into his. He gently pulled her closer to him, then he reached over the railing and picked her up and carried her over to the bench she had left her backpack under. She was as light as a feather in his arms, but he realized she had the strength of her mother in her. Both of them protected themselves, and the ones they loved, in the only way they knew. In running away, she was screaming for help in dealing with the pain she was in, the pain of having to realize that grown-ups were flawed, too, and the ones who swore to protect you were not always up to the job. Alexander prayed for the wisdom to be able to explain things to her, and he took a deep breath while he held her close on his lap. He unconsciously began to rock, forwards and backwards. The movement seemed to soothe her and her sobs became less frequent.

She wasn't looking up, as he rocked her like a baby. But he was. He saw Tegan and Patti walk in, followed by John and a younger man, who he figured must be Bill. They all froze when they saw him sitting and rocking the lost girl. He managed to raise one hand up to his lips and made the sign for quiet with his finger. Then he crooked it, to encourage them all to walk quietly over to where he waited for Katie to speak her pain.

"Do you want to tell me why you are here?" he finally asked her, when she became silent again and he felt her snuggle herself more deeply into his arms. By this time, all four of the other adults had gotten close enough to hear what she said. She spoke into his chest, but it was audible.

"I can't go home again. My mom hates me. I can't go to my dad's place. He's gay, and no one trusted me enough to tell me the truth. Everyone lies to me and I don't know who I can trust anymore." This came out in a quick rush, then she rubbed her tear-stained face into his very expensive shirt. "Can I come to live with you, *Tío Alejandro*?"

He looked up at the adults and saw the anguish on the faces of her parents that mirrored Katie's. And he knew he was now one of them. For better or worse, Katie now had three parents.

"Your mother doesn't hate you, Katie," he began, but she interrupted him.

"Then why did she hit me?"

"What were you doing, when she hit you?"

"We were arguing. She wouldn't tell me where she was after she got drunk on her birthday. And..." Katie's voice cracked. She took a deep breath before she continued in a small voice. "And I called her something bad."

Defensively, she continued. "She drank so much she got sick. She spent the night with some men. She did just what she's always warning me *not* to do. She's such a hypocrite!"

He heard a small sob from Tegan and he shook his head at her.

"No, Katie, your mom is not a hypocrite. She has been trying to protect you from the truths that might hurt you, for a long time. But I think you are old enough to hear the truths now, don't you?"

"What truths?" She looked up at him, still unable to see the other adults there, because her face was still in the circle of his arms.

Alexander took a deep breath. "You already know that your dad is gay? That Bill is more than a roommate to him, right?"

She nodded. "Kevin told me he thought they were, but I told him he was a liar. He likes Bill, but he's afraid it means he will be, too. That's why he plays all of those violent games all of the time. He says he needs to learn how to be a real man."

Tegan and John exchanged looks, and Alexander swore he could hear ice melting between them.

"What if I told you your mom was with only one man on her birthday? And the one man is someone who loves her very much and wants to marry her and spend the rest of his life taking care of all of you. How would you feel about that?" he held his breath.

She looked up at him. "How do you know?"

He looked into her eyes and smiled. "Because I'm the man."

She gave him a considering look. "You're not lying to me, too, are you? Saying that just to cover up for her?"

He laughed and felt the tension leave his body as he hugged her closely.

"No, sweetie. I love your mom and I love you. And I suppose I'll get to love Kevin, too, after he stops testing me to be sure I'm good enough for his mom." He kissed the top of her head.

"Do you think you might be willing to go home now?" he asked her.

She shook her head. "No, but I am really hungry. Are there any good pizza places around here?"

"In this neighborhood? Oh, God, yes! And I live really close by here. Why don't we go to my place and have some delivered? Then maybe you will be willing to go back home, after we have all have a chance to talk some more."

Katie froze. "*All*?"

Alexander lifted his arm and helped her to sit up straighter. She looked up at the assembled adults and her lower lip started to tremble again.

Tegan looked like she was about to cry. She spoke first. "Katie, I'm sorry I hit you. Please forgive me."

With a cry, Katie jumped off of Alexander's lap, and ran over to hug her mom. "And I'm sorry I called you a slut, Mom! I didn't mean it. I love you."

Alexander raised his eyebrows at Patti. "Slut?"

Patti clarified. "Alcoholic slut." She shook her head disparagingly. "They grow up so quickly these days."

John approached the hugging pair. "Katie? I'm sorry we lied to you. He's right. We were just trying to protect you."

Katie looked up at him, and sniffled. "Honestly, Dad. I'm not a child anymore. Bill could have told you that."

She turned to look at Bill. "In fact, why didn't you?"

He rolled his eyes at her. "I tried, honey, really I did. But he still sees you as his little girl."

She made a face at her dad. "I'll always be your little girl, Dad."

She let go of Tegan, who reluctantly let her go and she walked over to hug her dad, who promptly started to cry as he held her.

Alexander took that opportunity to take Tegan in his arms and she melted against him, as if she needed his strength to stay upright.

He held her closely and stroked her hair, her shoulders, then purposely restrained himself from stroking anywhere else, mindful of the baleful eye of Katie, who watched them over her dad's arm.

He tilted Tegan's face up. "How'd I do, on fatherhood one-oh-one?"

She smiled at him through her tears. "Birth by fire, huh? Better than I ever dreamed possible. You were born to be a dad."

He smiled at her. "Comes from being the oldest, I guess. Now, what's say we all get going to my place, and order some pizza? I'm starved! Emotional trauma takes a lot out of you, and it sure makes you hungry!"

Patti made a face at Tegan. "*Most* of us, anyway. I'll drive John and Bill in my car. You take Tegan and Katie. You lead, I'll follow. You seem to be really good at that today."

There was some throat clearing, then everyone started to laugh in relief and they left the zoo to go eat.

Fifty-two

Patti wasn't the only one who was truly impressed by Alexander's condo. Tegan had grown used to its opulence, and John and Bill were quieter about their admiration. But Katie was ecstatic, wandering around from room to room, loudly exclaiming about and enjoying the artwork, the view from the balcony and the plush carpeting she kept wiggling her bare toes through. She loved the Jacuzzi and the king-sized water bed. Patti's eyebrows went up into her hair when she first saw that and she turned to look at Tegan, who blushed deep red, shrugged, then laughed.

Later, after they had all eaten their fill of pizza, with cokes all around, they sat back on the couches near the fireplace and relaxed. Katie was still walking around admiring the artwork, while the adults smiled at her indulgently.

Finally, she walked back over to stand in front of Alexander, who was sitting on the futon with Tegan. He was having a difficult time keeping his hands off of her and was mentally counting the minutes until he could pick her up the next night and drag her back to ravish her on that same futon, once again.

He leaned over to place a quick kiss on her ear and whispered, "I live for tomorrow night."

She turned to look at him and she smiled at him with love. At that moment, Katie began to speak to them, with her hands on her hips.

"So, *Tío Alejandro*, you really expect me to believe you are willing to give up all of *this*?" She waved her arms around at the richly-decorated condo, "For a crappy little house in the suburbs, with my mom and two kids who are going to test you until we get tired, then rest up and test you some more? We are going to irritate the hell out of you and try to break you. And that's what you want?"

Alexander shook his head at her and frowned. "What did your mother tell you about swearing, Katie? Not until you are eighteen and moving out of the house. It's okay around your friends, but we are *not* your friends. We are your parents, and we love you. But do not swear where we can hear it."

She gave him a considering look. "You didn't answer my question."

"Yes. I'm going to marry your mother and you can come along when we look at houses, to be sure we can find a bigger one that won't be so crappy to you. And as for the testing you two are going to do? Bring it on, girlie. There were eight after me. I can take it. And I can dish it back at ya. Just ask all of my nieces and nephews."

She smiled at him. "Okay, then. I approve."

She ran back over to the balcony, to see where the loud music drifting up from the street was coming from.

Tegan gave Alexander an odd look. "You know, I realize it's just a technicality at this point, but you *still* haven't asked me if I want to marry you!"

He raised his eyebrows at her and kept looking at her, while he said, "Patti? Are you still willing to watch Katie and Kevin for us tomorrow night?"

"Of course!" she said.

John cleared his throat. "I was hoping I could spend some time with them tomorrow night. I think Bill and I really need to sit down with them, especially Kevin, and talk some things out."

He turned to Tegan, "I know it's not one of my visitation weekends. But do you think that would be okay with you?"

She nodded. He let out a sigh of relief. "Good. Now I just need to try to think of how we are going to answer all of their questions."

Alexander cleared his throat. "Well, if you want some scientific stuff to back you up, I know some really good websites."

At John's surprised expression, he smiled. "My baby brother, Roberto. Amazing how quickly prejudices vanish when it's someone you love, huh?"

John smiled at him. "Thanks. For everything."

Alexander returned his smile. "You're welcome."

He turned back to Tegan. "So, girl. You need to put on your dancing shoes tomorrow night. We are going out on the town. And there just might be something important I'm going to want to ask you. Not that I'm giving you any hints at all, but you had better be ready to give me an answer and it had better be the answer I want. I have ways of convincing you, you know." He leered at her. She blushed again.

They realized just how late it was getting and Alexander offered to drive Tegan and Katie back home so he could meet Kevin. Patti first drove John and Bill home, then she headed back to their neighborhood. They returned to find there were streamers all over the O'Neill trees and "Katie, we love you" signs had been posted everywhere. The neighbors ran out to hug everyone in sight and there were very few dry eyes, while everyone welcomed Katie back to where she belonged.

Fifty-three

A month later, when the kids were spending another weekend with their dad and Bill in the city, Tegan tapped her foot while she sat on the side of the Jacuzzi and waited. Impatiently, she looked at her watch for the hundredth time and finally, she jumped up and looked at the tiny plastic square and looked again.

Then she yelled, "Alex! Come in here! I need you right now!"

Alexander, who had been getting breakfast ready, came at a run, afraid she had fallen or somehow hurt herself.

He burst through the door and, panting, grabbed her. "What is it? What's wrong, my love? What do you need?"

She gave him the little plastic square. "That's what. I need you right now. And for the next eighteen years."

He looked at the square and a look of unholy joy lit his face. "You are?"

She nodded at him and he picked her up and twirled her around the room, then he put her down and kissed her, thoroughly and repeatedly.

Finally, he stopped long enough to talk to her, saying sternly, "That's it, young lady. No more alcohol for you. I've waited too long for this moment. I'm so happy I could explode. Maybe I won't drink anything either, in solidarity with you? How's that? I wonder if it will be a girl or a boy. I don't care, but I'd like another one of each, i that's okay with you. *¡Dios mío!* I'm going to be a daddy!"

She patted the side of his face. "You already *are* a daddy."

He looked at her and smiled. "No, I'm *Tío Alejandro*. That's wha your kids call me and that's all right with me. They already *have* daddy. But now we have to move the wedding plans up. No baby o mine is going to be born a bastard. I know I'm old-fashioned, bu there you are. So when are you due?"

She shrugged. "Probably in December sometime. I'll get a due date when I go to the OB."

He nodded. "Then let's get married in September. In fact, no matter what day of the week it is, how about on the nineteenth o September?"

He leered at her and smiled at the surprised look on her face. "Yes I remember to the minute the first time I touched you. It's appropriate we get married exactly one year to the day, from the day you changed my life with a dance."

He grabbed her to hold her close to his heart, saying in a worried tone, "Hey, I have no experience in this sort of thing. We don't have to stop making love, just because you are pregnant, do we? I mean maybe once the kid gets so big there isn't enough room for him *and* me in there anymore? But for now?"

She smiled at him, shaking her head. "No reason in the world we have to stop doing what got us in this position in the first place. And September nineteenth is just fine with me. You are *such* a romantic! I love you, Alexander Reyes."

He stopped trailing kisses down her neck to whisper into her ear. "What position is that, soon-to-be-*Señora* Reyes? Do you have any special requests, or is it okay if I pick one?"

She laughed, feeling her toes curl and chills run down her spine once again. "Only one? How about two or three of my favorites, then two or three of yours? By then breakfast will be so burned, we'll have to go out to eat. Then we can come back here and start all over again, playing our favorite game."

He picked her up, carried her over to the waterbed and dumped her unceremoniously into the middle of it. Then he picked up a remote control unit and suddenly the room was filled with the Santana song, "Game of Love." Michelle Branch sang, "Tell me, just what you want me to be... one kiss, and 'boom' you're the only one for me..."

He smiled at her, as he moved over to cover her body with his. "*¡Mi querida!* This is the song we will do our first married dance to, at the wedding."

She sighed with contentment as they began to move together again.

"Didn't you tell me Edgar said women make up the rules, and men have to learn them and follow them?"

He nodded, then resumed licking and sucking his favorite places.

She had that dreamy, aroused look on her face he loved to see so much, as she said, "Why don't we do it our way and write the rules to our own private 'Game of Love' ourselves... together? That way we can play it *our* way."

He looked up from what he was doing. "You win. I win. Sounds good to me. Let's play again."

And they did.

Meet

Fiona McGier

I have been an avid reader my whole life. And I have always "written" stories in my head, when bored, or occupied with some other task like baking or cooking. I used to think that everyone had characters "talking" to them all of the time. My 4 kids learned early on that when Mom had "that look" on her face, to not interrupt what I was doing. A couple of years ago, I finally decided that my head was getting too "crowded", and that some of these people and their stories had to be written down. I feel like they are telling me their secrets, and then once the book is done, they are happy to have been heard, and they are quiet. I have always enjoyed romances, and hope that you find my characters to be as interesting as I do.